CHIMÆRA

THE INFINITY ENGINES: ORIGINS

ANDREW HASTIE

Copyright © 2018. Andrew Hastie

The right of Andrew Hastie to be identified as the Author of the Work has been asserted by him in accordance with the Copyright, Design and Patents Act 1988.

All rights reserved.

No part of this publication may be reproduced, stored in a retrieval system, or transmitted, in any form or by any means without the prior written permission of the Author, nor be otherwise circulated in any form of binding or cover than that in which it is published and without a similar condition being imposed on the subsequent purchase.

All characters in this publication are fictitious and any resemblance to real persons, living or dead is purely coincidental.

4.5

May 2018

To my beautiful wife and daughters, thank you for everything

and mum, for being so strong.

A x

1
ARCHANGEL

Michael had been named after an angel.

His mother was a staunch Catholic who loved the stories of the saints and had read them to him every night in bed. Until when, at the age of eight, Michael discovered comics like 2000AD, and so ended his religious education.

It was a popular name in Ireland; there were two other boys in his class named after the leader of Heaven's army. But Michael had always preferred his other role — the angel of death.

His father worked nights as a taxi driver. Leaving them every evening with his flask of coffee and Tupperware box of sandwiches to trawl the streets of Ulster in his black cab.

Every morning, just before his father came home, Michael would wake and wonder if this was the day he would kill him.

When he was thirteen, his father had started to bring home presents for his mother — pieces of jewellery that he'd 'taken as payment', he told them once at the breakfast table as he opened the whisky.

It was a strange existence, getting ready for school while your father was winding down from a night shift. He would sit and chat with them over cornflakes, getting mildly drunk. Then when his eyes began to glaze over he would go and watch the football he'd recorded on a VHS from the night before — no one was allowed to tell him the result. He considered that a mortal sin.

At first Michael hadn't paid much attention to the gifts because they seemed to make his mother so happy, but over the next two years he began to notice a pattern — he couldn't help it; there was something in the way his dad acted just before another gift appeared. He got snappy, agitated and aggressive for no reason, and then after the gift appeared, he would turn into a different person altogether. Michael would never forget the day his mother asked him to help her put one of the necklaces on — it was as if God was showing him the way.

The moment he touched the golden chain something exploded inside his head. It was like a firework of images fizzing around in his mind, their trails spinning around in front of his eyes.

They were the random memories of a stranger, one moment in a pub, the next outside the kebab shop on Dock Street waiting for a bus. Everything was jumbled and out of sequence. Michael thought he was having some kind of religious vision until his purple-faced father appeared, his eyes wild with rage as he tried to strangle him.

Michael dropped the necklace and ran out through the garden and up into the back field. When he reached the stream he threw up.

Sitting on the bank, watching his breakfast float slowly away between the watercress and the plastic bottles, Michael wondered if it could have been some kind of revelation. That after all that praying, his mother had finally got her miracle; her only son had been blessed with visions.

Except it told him that his father was the Ulster Ripper.

It was late 70s in Northern Ireland, a time when the police were focused on dealing with the internal conflicts between the IRA and the Ulster Defence Force. No one seemed to have paid any particular attention to the disappearance of a string of young women, mostly prostitutes, from the streets of Belfast.

With patrols on permanent watch throughout the city, it seemed impossible to believe that someone would go on a killing spree, but Michael had been following the story for the last eighteen months. The papers would quickly lose interest in the gaps between the murders, but every time a new body was found on waste ground, his mother would receive another gift.

Michael had prayed to all the saints for guidance, but none had been forthcoming.

Until now.

2
MEMORIES

Caitlin had always thought of her life as divided into two halves: the innocent time while death was a mystery and life was full of wonder, followed by the painful reality of knowing.

Most other ten-year-olds were still puzzling over the existence of Santa Claus and the Tooth Fairy when she had to deal with the loss of her parents. 'Loss' was probably too weak a word; she hadn't misplaced them, they were taken from her on one seemingly normal Saturday in July.

The details of their last goodbye were burned into Caitlin's memory: the way they snapped at each other at the breakfast table, the sunlight that caught her mother's hair when she hugged her for the last time — holding her so tight she couldn't breathe.

Caitlin cherished every moment, again and again.

She stood in the garden of their old house and watched her younger self through the kitchen window as she waved goodbye to her parents. Tears rolled down her cheeks as Caitlin felt the heartache once more.

No one should put themselves through this, she told herself.

Grief and loss were supposed to dull with time, as the brain slowly filtered out the pain. But Caitlin had the benefit of time, or rather the ability to travel back through it. She could come back and open the wound in her heart whenever she felt like it, and did so far too often.

It had started as a way to remember them. Coming back here after the Dreadnoughts had officially called off the search — there were no bodies, no victims — other than herself. She could still feel the wet whiskers of her guardian, Rufius, sobbing as he held her, struggling to find the right words to tell her they were gone.

For a long time she refused to accept it. Viewing the same scene a thousand times from a hundred different angles, looking for any kind of clue, but it was always the same: her parents went off on their mission with a look of grim determination — the argument of the night before still hanging over them.

It was a terrible fight. One that she couldn't bring herself to revisit — she didn't have to, the memory of it was etched into her soul. Sitting halfway up the stairs, she shivered in her nightdress and stifled her cries into her teddy bear.

Raised voices had woken her from a dreamless sleep. At the time the words they used were complex, technical terms that her young mind couldn't process, but there was one thing her mother had said that would stay with her forever.

'She can't die, Thomas, we can't let her die!'

3
REPRIMAND

The Great Library of the Oblivion Order was vast, its stacks rising high up into an unseen ceiling hundreds of metres above. The collected knowledge of every civilisation in history was stored within it. Every book and manuscript, stone tablet or papyrus scroll had been tracked down and 'collected' for research by the Scriptorians, a guild of archivists responsible for safeguarding the written word.

Caitlin gazed up into the towering columns of books. She never ceased to be amazed by how the venerable 'Indexers' navigated the distant shelves with such grace and agility. Like trapeze artists they flew between the stacks with a consummate ease.

She noted the coloured robes of their colleges: scarlet marked a Mayerstein, while the cool blue of a Dewey was more rare and a Crimson denoted a master of the more obscure Ranganathan classification.

No one could agree on one indexing system. It had been fiercely debated for over a thousand years, which meant the library was in a permanent state of chaos — one that could only be mastered by many years of training, something she was only just beginning to come to terms with.

When she turned sixteen, Caitlin was allowed to select her guild. It had been a difficult choice. Many of her friends were either joining the ranks of the Copernicans, to study the paths of time and calculate possible futures, or opting for the more adventurous Draconians, her parents' guild, to explore the unknown areas of the forgotten past.

She couldn't bring herself to follow them. Although it was her birthright and her guardians had expected it of her, she chose to rebel — she opted to become a librarian, a member of the Scriptoria.

Her love of books began long before her parents' disappearance. The worlds she discovered within their pages were wondrous slices of history: from the medieval romances of the Vulgate Cycle, to the dark chronicles of the Spanish conquest, she would spend hours exploring the histories attached to them.

After they were gone, the manuscripts became a form of escape, gateways to secret places that helped her forget the grief, diverting her thoughts away from the loss.

She used the timelines of the books, their chronologies, to travel like no other teenager could imagine. It was a unique talent that only the members of the Oblivion Order could appreciate.

She was no ordinary seventeen-year-old. She could travel back through history.

Caitlin walked between the long rows of leather bound volumes, breathing in the aroma of old vellum, ink and thousands of years of study. She loved the ambience of the library, of being safe inside a labyrinth of ancient knowledge — each tome a portal to another age. She could spend many lifetimes in here and never have to deal with the harsh realities of the world outside.

Caitlin was still in her first year of training and already things weren't quite going to plan. The dissertation she carried under her arm was still unfinished; her tutor expected at least ten-thousand words today and she was closer to five. The problem was the subject he'd chosen: 'The indexing system of Grandmaster Mayerstein 11.250-11.301', was possibly the most boring and mundane thing she'd ever had to write about.

When she reached his office, the door was closed and Caitlin knocked gently, praying that he'd forgotten their appointment and gone out.

'Enter,' came the quick response, destroying any hope of postponement.

The offices of a Scriptorian master were supposed to be a reflection of their state-of-mind. Most were incredibly well organised and meticulously maintained: taking a certain pride in their small fiefdom. A stark contrast to the chaos of the greater library outside.

A master's personal collection was usually populated with the rarest of books, full of forbidden and archaic knowledge that older students would whisper about with a certain breathless awe.

However, this was not the case with her tutor, master Dorrowkind. An absent-minded, bumbling man who had trouble finding the glasses on the top of his head let alone the chronicles of Pliny the Elder.

Dorrowkind was a large man, around the waist rather than in height. His long grey hair was thinning and the aforementioned glasses were perched neatly on his creased forehead.

'Come in, come in,' he said, summoning her with a wave of the parchment he was examining. 'Excuse the mess. Having something of a sort out.'

She had never seen it tidy. As usual, the floor of the office was covered in books and papers, as was the large desk, the chairs and the spiral staircase that led up to his reading room.

Caitlin trod carefully between the priceless antiques, knowing that one misstep could damage any number of thousand-year-old documents that lay scattered across the Turkish rug.

'Makepiece,' said Master Dorrowkind with a sigh before slumping down into his chair.

Caitlin heard the chair creak under the weight and wondered how many more times he could do that before it gave way.

He opened a ledger and leafed through the pages of names until he found hers. 'Once again, you appear to have missed another of your study deadlines.'

She could see a grid of handwritten marks beside her name — there was more than one scarlet entry.

'Yes, I wanted to discuss the subject,' she said, holding up her dissertation.

'Finding it a bit dry by any chance?' Dorrowkind asked with a wry smile. 'The Mayerstein principles of archival are the bedrock of this institution.'

'Yes, I know, but it's just not something I —'

'So, I take it you've haven't come to hand in your final draft?'

She blushed. 'No.'

'You realise this is a compulsory requirement to pass the first year?'

'Yes, but —'

'No buts, Miss Makepiece. I don't make the rules. The indexing is a core curriculum subject. Not something that is open to negotiation.'

He leaned forward on his chubby elbows and extended a pale, fat finger. There was an unspoken rule about the wearing of gloves within the library — it was the exclusive privilege of a master to be able to remove them.

'I have to confess I've been deliberating recently over your suitability for the role of Scriptorian. You seem to lack the singular dedication for the systems of the collection. Without strict regulation of the indices we'll fall into chaos. The index is paramount!'

Caitlin thought it slightly hypocritical for him to question her ability to organise while sitting in the mess of what was clearly a hunt for a missing manuscript.

'But if I could just have a few more days, maybe a week?' she begged. 'I could help you find whatever it was you were looking for?'

The master's eyes glazed over, something that he did when his mind wandered — he'd obviously forgotten why he'd turned over his office.

Caitlin saw her chance. 'I've already worked through the twenty basic tenets of classification, but there were some elements that didn't make sense, so I've made some improvements.'

Dorrowkind coughed. 'Well, you certainly have your grandfather's spirit! How exactly do you propose to improve a system that's been used for over five hundred years?'

She put her notes down on his desk and rolled up the sleeves of her robe, exposing her long silk gloves. 'Let me show you what I've learned so far. Why don't I start on this while you read it?' She pointed to the unsteady piles of books behind her.

An hour later, she'd reordered the last of the shelves, using her own attribute-value system.

Dorrowkind put down her essay. 'Not bad, Makepiece,' he said, looking genuinely impressed, 'as far as it goes. I'll give you a seven-day extension to complete it.'

'Thank you, Master.'

He stood up and stretched his back, his belly protruding under the long scarlet robes. His chains of laddering jangled as they bounced off his huge stomach. They were obviously ceremonial, and the idea of him using them as he scaled the heights of the stacks like a bloated fairy made Caitlin smile.

He walked over to her neatly organised shelves of books and, after putting on an elegantly embroidered pair of cotton gloves, began studying their spines.

'I knew your grandfather well. A brilliant scholar and archivist — you've clearly inherited some of his talents. Yet I've never quite understood why you didn't follow your parents into the Draconians? You have their spirit and determination. I worry that you will find the Scriptoria too uninspiring — lacking in challenges.'

His eyes lit up as his finger hooked a small leather book out of the middle of the collection.

'Eureka!'

Caitlin could tell that their meeting was over. She was more than happy to avoid a discussion about why she'd chosen to be a bookworm rather than an explorer.

She left the master to his book and quietly closed the door.

4
CHAPTER HOUSE

[Fitzrovia, London. 11.860]

The Chapter House had been Caitlin's home for the last seven years. Located in Victorian London, the unassuming townhouse in the heart of Fitzrovia contained the nearest thing she had to a family.

Managed by Alixia De Freis and her husband Methuselah, it acted as both a hotel and a staging post. The entrance to the building may have been based in the nineteenth century, but many of the rooms and floors were actually located in different parts of history. This meant it was vastly bigger on the inside and frequented by an eclectic mix of travellers from different eras. Caitlin had grown up listening to extraordinary after-dinner stories about lost treasures, ancient civilisations and forgotten paths through time.

Master Dorrowkind was right about one thing at least — she loved tales of adventure.

Caitlin stepped out of the garden shed and into bright

sunshine. Alixia refused to allow the portal to the library any nearer the house, and had forced Methuselah to move it to the bottom of the garden.

It was strange to think that the small, nondescript wooden shack was a gateway to the largest collection of human knowledge in existence — not to mention the most useless assortment of broken lawnmowers in London.

'Cat!' exclaimed Lyra, as Caitlin walked into their lounge. 'What took you so long?'

'Dorrowkind lost something,' she said, raising her eyebrows and dropping her dissertation on the table. 'But, I've got an extension — another week.'

Lyra scowled. 'So you're not coming with us?'

She'd forgotten they were supposed to be going away. Lyra and her brother Sim had been planning to do the Grand Tour over the summer; a journey through some of the more unusual parts of history, starting with Tibet.

'I thought we could go over the itinerary tonight?' Lyra said, looking down at the neatly arranged row of unusual artefacts spread out on the old wooden trunk they used as a coffee table.

Caitlin picked up the seventh object. 'It's only a week, which still leaves six for our adventure.'

It was a metal singing bowl from a Tibetan monastery that was rumoured to be over nine-hundred-years old. Touching it with her bare hands she saw the history unravel in her mind. Ribbons of its timeline unfurled around her arm, revealing a map of its chronology. She could move through time using these paths. They called it 'weaving', and it was the safest way to navigate back into the past. The routes through history were notoriously complicated and full of dead-ends — redundant branches that you could get lost in for years.

'Not that one!' snapped Lyra, taking the bowl back. 'I want to meet the third Dali Lama.'

Suddenly, Sim walked in carrying a tray of teacups and cakes. 'Cat! How did the meeting go? By my estimation you had less than a twenty-three-point-four percent chance of success.'

Sim was lovely, if not a little geeky, and he was a Copernican which meant he spent all day working with probabilities and statistical analyses — everything he did was based on some kind of percentage.

'Better than expected,' she said smugly. 'He gave me another week and actually let me use my new system on his books.'

'Well played,' Sim said, placing the tray down on the table. 'You certainly have a knack for beating the odds.'

Lyra chuckled. 'Or manipulating men.'

'So we can't leave for another week?' Sim asked, sitting down on the other side of the table and pouring the tea.

Lyra surveyed the remaining objects and picked up a glass jar containing the bone of a human finger. 'I vote we drop the pilgrimage.'

'I spent three weeks getting that!' Caitlin protested, taking the ossuary away from Lyra. 'Do you know how hard it is to break into the Vatican?'

They both looked at her with mocking smiles. 'You only told us like a hundred times.'

'How did I know the Pope was keeping it in his bathroom!'

'It's not an image I want to keep,' Sim muttered.

'Anyway — the bones of St Augustin would have led to the missing bible of St Kitts. You know that was my best shot of getting a pass in restoration.'

Lyra tutted. 'Bookworm! You spend too long with your precious manuscripts. We want to have fun! I vote we drop the dinosaur hunt.' She picked up the flint axe.

They all agreed. No one was particularly interested in going back into pre-history. There was a limit on how far they could travel; ten thousand years was as far as anyone outside of the Draconians was allowed to go. Her father used to take her on camping trips to the end of the last ice age when she was a child.

It was also the end of the line when it came to the Continuum: a mathematical model the Copernicans developed to study the past and predict the best possible future.

Caitlin's stomach rumbled, reminding her that in her anxiety about the meeting with Dorrowkind she'd skipped lunch.

'What's for dinner?' she asked, picking up a plate and helping herself to a slice of Victoria Sponge.

Sim smiled and counted on his fingers as he did a quick mental calculation. 'Seventy-point-six percent chance of boar.'

'That's not even close!' Lyra squealed, sniffing the air. 'It's venison.'

5
SABIEN

Michael began to experiment and soon found that he had the ability to read other objects — a talent he decided to hide from his mother, who was such a devout Catholic she would probably have disowned him as a witch.

Unable to stand being in the house because of the visions of his father, he began to wander off into the woods behind their house. He soon discovered that he could 'read' the old oak trees, using their long, convoluted histories to move backwards in time — stepping back into ancient forests, and exploring forgotten epochs before man began to cultivate the land.

He was thirteen when he discovered his father was a serial killer. Not something that most teenagers imagine in their wildest, hormone-fuelled dreams. While his friends were comparing face fuzz and masturbatory fantasies about Nicole Adams in year eleven — he was following the news stories about dead girls.

It took him four years before he found the strength to do something about it.

The final straw had been when his father had turned on his mother. Somehow the harm he did to strangers was never as real, but when he hit his mother Michael realised that everything had obviously been a rehearsal for this final act.

His seventeen-year-old soul couldn't bear the weight of the guilt any longer and Michael took it upon himself to go back and stop him before it ever started.

He was holding a gun to his father's head when the man appeared out of thin air.

And he let him do it.

He simply watched as Michael shot his dad, kneeling in the woods and cursing all the 'Whores of Babylon,' like some evangelical pastor.

When it was over, the officer explained about the consequences of his actions; how he'd saved so many women, some of whom went on to have a positive effect on something called the 'Continuum'. He was very impressed with Michael's talents and sense of justice, offering him a position in the most unusual police force Michael Sabien could have imagined.

It was only after he was initiated into the Order that he discovered he was quite unique. Someone who could use 'organics' like wood and stone was thought to be a freak, and Michael quickly learned to hide his talent. But he soon discovered that the Protectorate was the perfect vocation for a loner, especially one that had an affinity with serial killers.

6
MUSÆUM

[Egypt. Date: 9.780]

The best part of her training was the vocational placement. Caitlin had opted to work at the Musaeum of Alexandria, which housed the famous Royal Library.

Located in Egypt, 9.780 — using the Order's Holocene calendar, 220 BC to the uninitiated — it was a wondrous place, filled with the collections of the Ptolemaic dynasty. A centre of learning and research that had been home to the great thinkers such as Archimedes and Euclid, the library had weathered centuries of turmoil and conflict before finally burning down during Caesar's civil war.

A large contingent of Scriptorian researchers were stationed at the Musaeum; collating and documenting the ancient materials and using them to travel back to verify their sources. The library was a cross between a university campus and a departure lounge; a terminus that branched out into thousands of unexplored parts of history. Nearly everyone that worked there was either a student or a journeyman on their way to some remote part of antiquity.

The dry Egyptian summers meant that the papyrus scrolls were like tinder, creating a serious fire risk — made worse by the numerous oil lamps and candles that were used for lighting. The Scriptorian firefighters were always easy to spot in a crowd; they were the most stressed-out people she'd ever seen.

For Caitlin the most intriguing part of the collection was the maps. Just as it was with books, charts from every ship that had ever visited the port of Alexandria were meticulously copied and stored in the lower levels. Long, dark tunnels had been bored through sandstone into a large natural cavern where the master stonemasons had carved a giant map of the world as they knew it across the floor. The 'Mappa Mundi' was over twelve metres wide and forty metres long — and it was completely wrong.

Without the benefit of satellite photos or a decent system of longitude — time-keeping being something of an issue before the seventeenth century — the ancient cartographers had relied on the observations of navigators. Ships were totally reliant on good charts, but their perspective was biased. Coastlines and soundings were drawn from the point of a boat rather than a bird's eye view.

Caitlin adored the artistry these naive mapmakers applied to their visions of the world. Their struggle to understand the true shape of the planet fascinated her. It was hard to imagine living in a time when continents like America and Australia didn't exist, and when the earth wasn't even thought to be round.

The curator of maps was a Scriptorian by the name of Arsenius Zillers. He was an old man who'd chosen to spend his retirement in the Royal Library working on one of his favourite topics: the 'Maps of the Ancient Sea Kings'.

Zillers was always to be found pottering around in the basement, trying to trace the provenance of rare and unsigned charts. Caitlin had spent many hours helping him determine the authentic originals from the blatant copies — her favourites were always those that just plainly made it up.

'Ridiculous!' Zillers would exclaim, holding up a depiction of some part of Europe that resembled a misshapen bear's head rather than a country. They would laugh and move on to the next. She loved it when he discovered something unusual, which didn't happen often, but when it did his eyes would light up like a child on Christmas Day.

His theory of the 'Sea Kings' was based on a chart discovered by Piri Reis, an Ottoman admiral, in the sixteenth century.

The Piri Reis map illustrated the coastline of Antarctica, something that hadn't been seen for over ten-thousand years. It had been totally ignored until a ground radar study carried out in the twenty-first century by the Canadian Air Force had shown the map was incredibly accurate.

It was an anomaly, something that even the Draconians couldn't explain. Zillers, who had been an administrator in the records department, had just lost his wife and found something fascinating about the mystery. He decided to take early retirement and spend what was left of his life searching for the answer, and it had led him to Alexandria — a research position that seemed to agree with him.

'Good evening Miss Makepiece,' greeted Zillers, looking up from his chart table as Caitlin entered.

'Master Zillers,' she replied, and bowed.

He was an old man and his health was declining. His skin was dry, paper-like and with a tinge of yellow, and years of pouring over books in bad light had ruined his eyesight, so that he relied on a magnifying glass to study his beloved charts. He also leaned heavily on a wooden staff when he walked.

Zillers put down his lens and took the cup of wine from her. It was his favourite: Black Laurel, a dark red from the Ionian Islands. In return for her assistance, he was helping her with the dissertation, or rather trying to keep her from getting expelled.

'So how went the meeting?' he asked, swirling the wine around and savouring the aroma.

They'd had many discussions about her 'improvements' of the Mayerstein index. Zillers was a good listener, although she'd never been able to convince him that hers was a better system.

'Master Dorrowkind let me reorganise his personal collection,' she said with pride.

Zillers' eyes twinkled. 'Did you use your new method?'

'Of course. I told him Mayerstein was flawed, but I don't think he's going to give me a pass.'

The old man smiled, like a proud grandparent at a prize giving. 'I will let you into a little secret. You aren't supposed to complete it — it's a test, to show your strength of character. Those that do complete it are failed.'

Caitlin was confused. 'How come no one tells you this?'

'It's not the last secret you will have to keep as a Scriptorian,' replied Zillers thoughtfully, 'but it's the first, and once you know it, you cannot unlearn it. The first year is a test of character, not ability. The chances are you are already being earmarked for great things.'

Caitlin blushed a little.

'So, where were we?' Zillers asked, putting down his wine carefully and unrolling another chart.

'The map of the North by Ptolemy?'

He shook his head. 'I thought we'd start on the merchant shipping lanes of fourteenth-century Venice.'

She pulled a face.

'As you wish, but only if you can tell me what is so strange about the "Camera map" of 11.502?'

'It uses a spherical grid, even though everyone still thought the world was flat,' Caitlin said with a knowing grin, and sat down on one of the tall stools — *it was going to be a good night*, she thought to herself.

7
DELAWNEY

[New York. Date: 11.876]

The mirror was dark; the silvering had blackened with age, and it was like looking into a pool of midnight.

Eleana Delawney shivered as she watched her reflection disappear, then knelt before the book and began the next part of the incantation.

The *Codex Arcanuum* was rare, one of only three that had ever been printed. Written by Johannes Belsarus, it was a seventeenth-century occult manuscript that she'd paid over a million dollars to possess specifically for this one spell.

Ever since she'd met Madame Blavatsky, Eleana's life had been dedicated to the study of ancient wisdoms. The mystical arts intrigued her; she studied Hermeticism, Theosophy, Qabalah and many other occult philosophies, but none had given her what she craved.

She had become obsessed with death and what lay beyond, attending séances and consulting spiritualists to try and find the answer to the eternal mystery, but they were all charlatans and tricksters.

No one could reach her husband, Felix.

He had died of tuberculosis five years after they were married in 1842. He was a brave man who had hidden the illness from her throughout their courtship. Following their lavish wedding they had spent the next two years touring Europe, as was the fashion for socialites of New York at the time.

Felix was the son of a railway magnate, and his wealth had shown her parts of the world she could never have dreamed of in her small apartment in Brooklyn before they met.

She saw the Buddhas of Tibet, the thousand temples of Bagan, and many more sacred sites, and it had been the longest honeymoon in history according to the New York Times. She didn't care; she was twenty-one and in love.

It was on one of their last expeditions to the mountains of Tibet that they met Helena Blavatsky, a Russian aristocrat who'd gone in search of the 'Masters of ancient wisdom'.

The two ladies had spent time together while the men had gone fossil hunting. Blavatsky was a woman with an immense spiritual presence, and seemed to instinctively know things about Eleana that she'd never told another living soul, not even her husband.

She was also the one who told her how Felix was going to die and the ways in which she might be able to bring him back.

Now, as Eleana knelt before the long black mirror with the Codex open on the floor before her — the book that Helena had described forty years ago — she began to recite the words of summoning.

The surface of the mirror shimmered, and suddenly it was as if she were looking through a window onto another world. She saw the dark buildings and streets of a strange city; it left her speechless, and as she stuttered the vision faded. Focusing on the words once more she repeated the mantra until she felt the harmonics attune and the image returned.

A figure emerged from one of the buildings; the silhouette of a man walking towards her. Tears rolled down her cheeks as she forced herself to continue the summoning.

He was coming, her Felix, just as Madame Blavatsky had foretold — she had finally conquered death.

But as the figure neared the other side of the mirror, her words caught in her throat.

The long claws of the nightmarish creature punctured the surface of the glass and grasped her neck. It lifted her off her knees as it stepped into the room. A creature with no eyes or nose, just a gaping mouth with hundreds of teeth.

'Felix,' she whispered mournfully as she felt its grip tighten.

8
BOB

Alixia De Freis was one of those people that always instinctively knew the right thing to do. Ever since Caitlin had come to live with her family she'd been a voice of reason. Always the perfect hostess, Alixia ruled the Chapter House like a Victorian governess — stern when she needed to be, but with a motherly affection that a frightened ten-year-old had found reassuring.

Rufius had tried his best, but he was an old man who'd spent his life in the field, and had no idea how to deal with the emotional needs of a young girl. Alixia made her feel like one of the family the moment she walked through the door. She was the nearest thing that Caitlin had to a parent, and she loved her dearly.

Yet Alixia was no ordinary lady — some would even say she was eccentric. One of her unique qualities was an obsession with saving extinct species. She loved all things botanical and had cultivated a beautiful roof garden of pre-historic plants and flowers that rivalled the herbariums at Kew, which was in fact where her husband, Methuselah, had borrowed the entire glass house that enclosed it.

Caitlin had gone to the roof first, but finding no one except Alixia's Dodo Maximillian rooting through the undergrowth for grubs, she made her way down to the baths.

The baths were one of Methuselah's greatest achievements. He was a temporal architect, an Antiquarian by guild and the genius who had developed the techniques that linked moments of architecture together — creating an infinitely expandable building.

The baths were from the Byzantine. A large lagoon of azure water, warmed by natural volcanic springs, steamed inside an ancient cavern that stretched far off into the distance. Decorated with the finest Roman mosaics and water fountains, it had all the trappings of the pre-Christian era, and it was deep, very deep. As children, Caitlin remembered how Lyra and Sim would scare each other with stories of the bodies that had floated up from the submerged village that lay far below the surface.

The baths were currently off-limits because of the Plesiosaurs that Alixia was nurturing.

Caitlin found her standing in the shallows, her skirt soaked to the waist and with a bucket of chopped tuna under one arm, feeding the most vicious looking dolphin she had ever seen.

'Now then, Bob,' she scolded in her mild French accent. 'No snatching.' She tapped him on the snout and he blasted a stream of water out of his blowhole in response.

'Hi,' Caitlin said, announcing herself.

'Ah Caitlin, bon soir. Come, help me with this ridiculous creature.'

Long rows of teeth loomed up over Alixia as her gauntleted arm dropped a lump of pink meat onto its tongue. The stench from his open mouth made Caitlin gag.

'No, you're okay. I've only just had dinner.'

Bob's tail splashed and sent a wave of water out into the pool, which grew as it moved away, crashing over the nearest fountain that was at least two metres high.

'Enough!' Alixia clapped her hands, and Bob sank slowly back below the surface. His cold, dark eyes disappeared last, leaving Caitlin with the distinct impression he was watching her.

'So, you didn't come to feed my fish,' Alixia said, handing Caitlin the bucket. She took off her long gauntlets and dumped them into the empty pail. 'What's on your mind?'

Alixia always had an uncanny ability to cut through the niceties and get to the heart of a problem.

'Do you ever wonder whether I should've joined the Draconians?' Caitlin asked, putting the bucket to one side.

Alixia pursed her lips, something she always did when she was concentrating. 'Have you suddenly fallen out of love with your books?'

Caitlin shook her head.

'Hmm, then maybe you've fallen out with you teacher?'

'I don't think Master Dorrowkind likes me very much.'

'You're too clever for him, I think. He spends too long in comfortable chairs reading about a life he's never had.'

Caitlin smiled. Alixia was cynical of most academics, especially ones that never bothered leaving the safety of their office.

'He gives me the most boring subjects. I'm sure the other students haven't been asked to write up the merits of indexing systems.' Caitlin was careful not to mention what Zillers had told her about the test.

Alixia smiled. 'Ah yes, that would be Mayerstein. Have you tried to change his mind about it by any chance?'

Caitlin folded her arms, watching Bob slowly glide off into the deep. 'I might have.'

Alixia nodded. 'But what did you really want to do?'

'Throw it back in his face and tell him it was a waste of time and show him the work I've been doing in Alexandria.'

'Just so. The next time you see him, be yourself and trust your instincts. You may still become a Draconian one day. But if not, your mother and father would still be as proud of you as I am.'

She put her arms around Caitlin and hugged her tightly.

'Now let's get out of here before Bob thinks there's a second course.'

9

MURDER

[Egypt. Date: 9.780]

After dinner, Caitlin made her excuses and went back to the Royal Library in Alexandria.

She had to steady herself against the rough wall as she descended the stairs into the chamber of maps. It was darker than usual and she had to concentrate on the uneven steps as she tried not to spill his wine.

Zillers was nowhere to be seen. The room was dark and cold, like a tomb. Many of the oil lamps had gone out or were spluttering as they ran low, which was highly unusual: he hated the dark and made a point of keeping the oil topped-up.

Walking across to the large chart table, Caitlin found his beloved maps strewn across the floor, scattered like a child's drawings after a tantrum.

She carefully placed the goblet on the table and removed her gloves. Touching the nearest chart with a fingertip, she hoped to glean something from its recent history. Her finger met a dark, sticky stain and she immediately snatched her hand away.

It was blood, and she could sense the violence of how it had got there.

A low groan came from one of the antechambers. Caitlin held her breath and quietly moved towards it.

In the flickering lamplight, she saw bloodstains on the floor and other signs of a struggle; broken furniture and scratches etched into the flagstones where something heavy had been dragged across the floor.

Her heart was beating hard against her chest as she moved closer to the alcove. The groaning had stopped, replaced with something more guttural, like an animal feeding.

Caitlin suddenly realised she had nothing to defend herself with. Looking around for a weapon, she saw Zillers' staff leaning up against the wall next to his cloak. The oak felt hard and heavy in her hand; it wasn't deadly, but it was better than nothing.

Gripping the stick tightly she rounded the corner and stopped cold.

Before her, kneeling over the body of Zillers, was a creature from a nightmare. A dark twisted thing with leathery skin covered in scars, like a burns victim. She watched dumbstruck as its claws raked at the old man's chest — carving something into his skin.

Caitlin dropped the staff, the sound echoing off the walls as it clattered across the floor. The creature's head turned slowly, twisting towards the noise. It had no eyes, only the long slit of a mouth and a grisly hole where the nose should have been.

Caitlin couldn't breathe, but could feel every one of the hairs on the back of her neck standing on end and her palms slick with sweat. The staff rolled into a corner and fell silent. Every muscle had frozen, her brain refusing to function. Nothing had prepared her for the paralysing fear — all those countless hours training with Rufius, learning how to defend herself — and she stood like an idiot trying not to wet herself.

The creature extricated itself from Zillers' corpse and turned towards her. It looked like it had once been human, but its body was terribly disfigured, holding itself more like a predator than a man. The slit of its mouth broke open revealing rows of long crystalline teeth as a low growl rumbled from its throat.

Caitlin braced herself for the attack; she wanted to close her eyes, but something stopped her — some insane part of her knew she had to watch this. It wasn't about dying. The analytical part of her brain was desperately trying to classify what was going to kill her instead of working out how to escape.

As the monster crawled towards her, she forced herself to reach for the tachyon on her wrist. It was so close that she could taste the stench of death as she hit the homing button and the world twisted away.

10

BACK HOME

[Chapter House, Date: 11.860]

'You cannot go to the Protectorate,' Methuselah declared, crossing his arms, 'unless you want to spend the next ten years in Bedlam.'

Sim's father was a striking man. The son of a Portuguese pirate and an Arabian princess, he was olive-skinned with short, black curly hair, a forked beard and dark brown eyes. When he smiled, the bright jewel embedded in his front tooth would light up the room.

'But what about Master Zillers? I was the only witness,' Caitlin said, sobbing, her tears flowing uncontrollably down her face. 'Who's going to tell them what happened?'

Methuselah dismissed her with a wave of his hand. 'The Protectorate have their own methods,' he said, tapping a scar that ran down the side of his face. 'We tell them nothing for now. I will send a message to Rufius, as he will know what to do. In the meantime you stay in the house.'

He kissed the top of her head. 'Lyra can help to ease

your pain, my lindeza.' He turned to Sim and his sister. 'Take care of her.'

They came and sat either side of Caitlin on the sofa, each putting an arm around her. No one spoke — they didn't need to, their friendship was all she needed right now.

Caitlin was no stranger to death; she had witnessed the carnage of historical battles, observed the catastrophic effects of pandemics like the black death, but somehow it was different when it happened to someone she knew.

Travelling through history was like watching a movie — albeit one that you were taking part it. No matter how real it was, you always had the reassurance that it had already happened, that you weren't responsible for the things that occurred.

Caitlin couldn't shake the feeling that she'd let Zillers down, that there was something she could have done to save him, even though she had no idea what is was. She'd contemplated jumping back a few hours and warning him, but she wasn't sure he would have believed her and the Order had a hundred different laws about changing the outcome of an event.

Tears dropped onto the watch face of her tachyon and she wiped them away. It was something that every member of the Order was required to wear; the tachyon not only allowed the Draconian rescue team to locate you anywhere in the timestream, but also acted as a homing device and get-out-of-jail-free card, which had saved her life more than once. There were two buttons on the side; one took you back two minutes in time, the other took you 'home' to whichever temporal location you'd bookmarked that to be.

The one she wore was given to her by her grandfather. A family heirloom, it was a MKII, which meant it didn't have all the new functionality of the latest MKIV, but she couldn't bring herself to upgrade it. Her grandfather had been

Caitlin's last living relative, and the grandmaster of the Scriptorians. His death was a peaceful affair, surrounded by his beloved books.

'Would you like me to assuage you?' Lyra whispered, brushing Caitlin's hair back off her face. She was a seer, and although only fourteen-years-old, one of the most promising in the Order. She could 'read' people, the way Caitlin could with objects. Lyra would look into your personal timeline and 'see' potential futures. It wasn't something that could be taught — she was born with it.

Caitlin sniffed and nodded. She wanted the horrible image of the creature out of her head, or at least the fear and horror that surrounded the memory reduced. Lyra could do that. Her abilities made her a skilful healer, and she'd helped Caitlin come to terms with the grief of losing her parents. Although there were still areas of that memory that even she hadn't managed to reach.

Lyra sat back and let Caitlin lay her head on her lap. Sim moved out of the way so she could put her feet up, and as Lyra began to stroke her temples, Caitlin felt her mind gently caressing the surface of her consciousness.

'Just relax, and listen to the sound of my voice.'

Two hours later, Sim returned with two steaming mugs of hot chocolate.

'Feeling better?' he asked with a look of concern.

'Yes, thanks,' Caitlin said and smiled, taking the mug with two hands.

'That was some crazy-arsed demon!' Lyra said, stretching her arms behind her head in a way that shouldn't have been physically possible.

Sim, who was obviously desperate to know all the gory details, sat down and rubbed his hands together. 'So?'

'It was like something from a fire, the skin was puckered and scarred,' Caitlin began.

'A Malevolent,' Sim interrupted.

'What?'

'An elemental from the maelstrom, draws its energy from fire — did it have glowing red eyes?'

Caitlin shook her head, and took a deep breath and continued.

'There were no eyes at all, just teeth — a lot of teeth — and a hole where its nose should have been.' She paused. Lyra's work was good but not perfect, and recalling the memory still held of tinge of anxiety, though nothing like the terror she'd felt before.

'Go on,' Sim urged.

'Sim!' Lyra snapped. 'Give her a break.'

'It's okay,' Caitlin said calmly. 'The creature looked like it had once been human; same number of arms and legs, but it prowled around on all fours.'

'Like a cat?' Lyra walked over to the bookshelves and began to browse the old leather tomes.

'No, more like an ape — except with really long claws, and horns.'

'Horns?'

'Bony protrusions, all along its spine and skull — and there was a terrible smell.' She gagged as the memory came back to her.

'Sorry, didn't manage to shut down the olfactory recall,' Lyra apologised.

Caitlin felt light-headed and physically sick.

Sim watched her skin turn grey and thought it best to change his line of questioning.

'So why would it want to kill a retired old master?'

'Maybe he was into demonology,' Lyra pondered, pulling a book off the shelf.

'Was he?' Sim asked Caitlin. 'Did he collect any maelstrom arcana? Do you think he summoned a demon?'

'He was kind,' said Caitlin, trying not to cry. 'A quiet, thoughtful man, but terribly sad. He lost his wife a few years back and decided to dedicate his life to research.'

Lyra handed her a tissue. The tears were streaming down her face without her knowing.

'So, he wasn't some kind of reaver on the quiet?' Sim asked, his analytical brain well suited to the role of amateur detective.

'How would I know?' Caitlin snapped.

'Enough!' said Lyra. 'It's taken me two hours to get her halfway normal. Don't undo all my good work by making her relive the whole thing again!'

'I think we should look into Zillers' past,' Sim declared, as if he had already made up his mind. 'No one just gets taken out by a demon like that.'

Lyra opened up a large, leather-bound grimoire she'd taken down off of the shelf.

'According to Trithemius it wasn't a demon,'

The engraved illustration was crude and rather artistic, but Caitlin felt herself shiver when she saw it.

The words across the bottom of the page read:

'Madrigor Satanus.'

11

SABIEN

[Alexandria, Egypt. Date: 9.780]

Inspector Sabien studied the body of the victim carefully. The man was clearly in his late seventies and showing all the signs of liver disease. Yellowing of the skin and pupils were clear indicators of cirrhosis, but the state of his liver was irrelevant compared to the huge open rents sliced into his chest.

The inspector took out his almanac and jotted down a series of notes. His initial impression of the crime scene were something he'd always found far more reliable than a photograph, not that he could have brought a camera back this far anyway. A temporal detective had to work within the restrictions of the era, as technology couldn't travel back past its original invention date.

Over the years, Sabien had learned to trust his instincts. There was something about the way certain things caught his attention when he first entered a crime scene that always proved useful to the case later down the line.

On this occasion, it was the wounds that bothered him.

They weren't made by a weapon, nor did they look savage enough to be that of an animal. Circling the body he thought they were reminiscent of a Chinese symbol. Sabien made a quick sketch of the shape they formed and put the notebook away.

Crouching down by the man's head, he examined the skull for damage. There were bruises by the temples and the lips had turned blue. Sabien had studied anatomy at the Sorbonne; the barber surgeons of pre-revolution Paris had taught him everything about the inner workings of the human body, and the ways in which it would decay.

The man had been dead less than twelve hours. His body was still in a rigid state; rigor mortis had contracted the muscles, stiffening them. Sabien took off one of his gloves and opened one of the corpse's eyes. There were signs of lividity and the skin was waxy and cold.

'Ten hours,' he noted to himself, putting the glove back on.

Standing up, he left the corpse and followed the trail of blood out into the map room, visualising the last moments of the man's life from the patterns of blood splatter.

There had obviously been a struggle, as the scattering of documents and charts indicated some kind of surprise attack — the man was working when the assault occurred. Blood trails lay on top of the discarded maps, lines of spray from arterial projections where a blade had entered his neck.

The assailant would have been incredibly strong. The victim weighed at least sixteen stone and would have been fighting for his life, yet the killer managed to drag him into the alcove. As Sabien looked back towards the body he saw the path clearly: the drag marks, the dislodged furniture, the torn charts — everything about the room matched his initial assessment.

Except for the staff.

The walking stick was half-hidden in the corner of the room, too far from the victim's cloak and hat. Its well-worn knob was a testament to how much the old man relied upon it. Sabien examined the wood carefully, looking for any sign that he might have used it to defend himself, but there was nothing — except for one bloody fingerprint.

This was his first substantial clue — imprinted on an object that could be used to go back to the precise moment of death. Although that wasn't strictly legal; there was a twenty-four hour exclusion zone in place around the murder — no chronology was supposed to be disturbed until the Copernicans had cleared the scene and granted them access.

Sabien knew he should wait until the forensics team arrived — that he should simply observe and document — but the SOCOs couldn't investigate organic evidence in the same way that he could.

Taking off his glove, he took hold of the stick and opened its timeline.

12

COPERNICAN ARCHIVES

The archives were deep below the Halls of Calculus. Sim had told Caitlin all about the Copernican headquarters and their steam-powered Difference Engine, a cathedral-sized computer that the statisticians used to calculate the complex probabilities of the future.

Sim was striding ahead of her as if he was on some kind of mission. Caitlin had to run to keep up with him as she followed him through the labyrinth of tall cabinets. There were thousands of rows of small wooden drawers, each one labelled with a brass-framed, handwritten card, which Sim read aloud as he went.

'Leyland, Lezzar, why did he have to be a Z?' he muttered to himself.

This was the almanac archive, the last resting place of every notebook ever used by an active member of the Order. Second only to the tachyon, the almanac was the most important tool that a member possessed. Part journal, part communications device, each almanac was tethered to a sympathetic twin that was held by the Copernicans, allowing them to maintain a constant channel of temporal information and a trackable object should one of the pair become lost.

As they passed the Ms, Caitlin wondered whether to ask about her parent's books, but there were literally hundreds of 'Ma' and Sim didn't seem in the mood for a diversion.

Earlier, when he'd suggested visiting the archive to retrieve Zillers' almanac from the archive, neither Caitlin nor Lyra had ever heard of it.

'It's not something we generally talk about,' explained Sim, blushing slightly. 'They record everything, every place you go, every note you make, and that can make people a little nervous — kind of big-brother-is-watching type of edgy.'

Lyra wasn't interested, and went off to do more research on the Madrigor, preferring to 'follow the beast rather than the victim.' Apparently, she knew someone in the Xenobiology department that might be able to shed some light on the creature.

'What about Methuselah's instructions?' Caitlin protested. 'I'm not supposed to leave the house.'

'It's not like you're roaming the streets,' he said, putting on his Copernican robes. They were dark purple, with multiple pockets sewn into the inner lining. 'Anyway, you'll be with me,' he added, tucking his almanac and brass slide rule into their respective pouches.

The Copernican headquarters was based in 11.547, a year that was determined to be suitably far enough away from the frontier — the present — to ensure the sensitive gearings of the difference engine was not affected.

Copernicans spent their days studying the millions of

variables that shape the timeline: calculating possibilities and eventualities to determine the best path into the future. Their computations were vast and took millions of hours to compute. Since one tiny adjustment to the past could make a massive change to the future, everything had to be simulated and then tested in the Continuum — a four-dimensional mathematical model that mapped every possible eventuality of the last twelve thousand years. Powered by the Infinity Engine, it was the epitome of temporal theory and only once an adjustment had been approved by the four separate oversight committees could a change be actioned. This process had been known to take as long as thirty years — giving them a reputation as slow and overly bureaucratic.

Since there were no electronics in the sixteenth century, everything was built from clockwork and powered by steam, which explained the vast size of the Hall of Calculus. The Infinity Engine, on the other hand, was a mysterious device, no bigger than a shoe box, and that only the most senior members of the Order, the Grandmasters, were allowed to access.

Except at your investiture.

On the day that each member was officially recognised by the Order, they were allowed to experience it.

Caitlin would never forget that day. Her mother and father had stood beside her as she placed her hand nervously into the carved wooden box. Nothing could have prepared her for what came next. To see the entire time continuum unwind around you, the millions of potential futures weaving into a single filament that stretched back over twelve thousand years. Every event that had ever occurred tagged and annotated with the temporal sigils of approval. For a nine-year-old it was like standing in the middle of your own private firework display.

When she finally took her hand out, the mark of the

Oblivion Order had been etched into her arm. The Ouroborous: a circled snake eating its own tail — painlessly burned into her skin forever.

'Zillers!' Sim declared finally, pulling open a drawer.
　　It was empty.

13

THE COLONEL

[Moscow. Date: 11.983]

Rufius Westinghouse was on his fourth cup of tea. The hot, sweet liquid was served in a gilded podstakannik, a small remnant of pre-communist Russia from a time of Tzars and winter palaces, and one of his favourite eras.

He sat in the small café reading the newspaper. His Russian was still bedding in; there hadn't been time to brush up properly, and the mission had been flagged as critical so Rufius improvised, 'borrowing' most of the lexicon from the local agent.

Known as 'intuiting', the process was common practice amongst the Order. It consisted of sharing memories, specifically around language, which was one of the most complex structures to impart to another and usually reserved for teachers who donated their brains after death — taking it from a living host tended to be a little messy.

From what he could make out the newspaper was mainly propaganda, with stories about how the 'evil empire' of the west was corrupt and preparing for war. Rufius was amused by a long article on how the US were using television to 'dominate the proletariat', showing a series of photos of children in a science lab with strange silver helmets strapped to their heads and watching Disney movies.

He took out his watch, being suitably old enough to prefer it on a chain rather than strapped to his wrist. The concentric dials on the tachyon were moving quickly, marking time in five different ways — the most important of which was counting rapidly down towards zero.

He smiled at the old waitress as she took away his tea glass and dropped a ten-ruble note onto the table. It was more than she would have earned in a month.

'Spend it wisely,' he said in Russian.

She eyed him with suspicion before quickly sweeping the note away into the folds of her apron.

'Thank you, Colonel,' she replied, observing the rank on his army uniform.

Rufius picked up his cap and gloves. He always preferred military roles, and there was something quite gratifying about the respect it inspired in the locals — it also made his job a lot easier.

'The telephone?' he asked politely.

She nodded to the back of the café, where a man was chatting away on an old Bakelite handset while rolling a cigarette.

'My husband,' she added with a look of disdain. 'Lazy bastard spends all day gambling on horses.'

Rufius donned his cap and pulled on his gloves, then took out a small pocketbook, his almanac, which contained the mission parameters.

'You're a Political Officer?' she asked nervously.

'No,' he assured her, tapping the insignia on his arm. 'Rockets.'

The hundreds of lines on her face relaxed a little;

worrying had aged her beyond her years. 'I'll tell him to get off the phone.'

Rufius nodded and opened the almanac and turned to his mission. Timelines flowed across its pages; branching flow charts and temporal equations constantly changed and updated as somewhere in the sixteenth century a Copernican team refined the minutest of parameters. He had less than three minutes to make the call, and by the look of their most likely outcome — save the world from nuclear devastation.

The waitress was berating her husband as Rufius went over to the phone. She ushered him away into the kitchen, the scolding still in full force as they disappeared through the bead curtain.

Deep within a bunker just outside of Moscow, a telephone rang, disturbing Stanislav Petrov, the duty officer of the early warning station who was staring at his screen in disbelief.

A satellite feed was showing five ballistic missiles heading towards the Soviet Union from the West coast of America. Alarms were ringing and the word 'LAUNCH' was flashing red on the monitor in front of him.

He knew he should inform the Kremlin; every second he delayed would lose valuable time for a tactical response — one that would initiate a massive retaliatory strike and begin World War III.

As the alarms sounded, he picked up the phone. 'Duty officer Petrov.'

'Comrade Petrov. This is Pionersky Radar Station. We are showing a false alarm on your system. Do you concur?'

A false alarm? Petrov glanced over to his radar screens. They were clear, showing no sign of inbound missiles. He felt the cold knot in his stomach relax as he realised how close he'd come to calling his commander.

'Thank you. I concur. Who is this?'

'Just a concerned comrade,' the voice said just before the line disconnected.

Rufius hung up the phone and checked the almanac one last time, watching the lines of destruction fading away.

Just as he went to close the book, a note appeared on the page.

'RW, need to speak to you urgently. MdF.'

It was Methuselah, which meant only one thing — Caitlin was in trouble again.

14

BAD PARKING

[Detroit, Michigan. Date: 11.922]

Henery Sergeant sat back in his seat and took a moment to admire his work. His designs for the Mark V were close to complete and tomorrow he would be ready to brief engineering and start building the first prototype.

As second draughtsman on the project, Henery's role was to ensure that it met the exacting requirements of the Antiquarian Standard — something that he took great pride in having helped define. The AS was a mark of quality, respected by every other guild within the Order. To the engineers it was a badge of honour and one that they all strived for — especially Henery.

He had drawn all of the plans himself, by hand, the specifications for each component meticulously documented and illustrated on hundreds of blueprints and diagrams.

The walls of his office were lined with ten years of work. Planning the next iteration of the tachyon, the most prized device of the Order, wasn't something to be taken lightly. The Mark IV had taken him eight years and had been one of the proudest achievements of his career, but this was to be his last, greatest work, and he wanted to make sure it was a masterpiece — even if it nearly cost him his marriage.

Henery suddenly realised how quiet the building had become — it was the middle of the night after all. He'd let the other members of the team go home, as they deserved a decent sleep after the all-nighters that they'd all worked over the last couple of weeks.

His shoulders were tense and knotted, aching from long hours bent over the plans. He kneaded them with his hands, rolling his shoulders to try and work out the tension. Henery was looking forward to getting back to his boat and spending some time on the lake. The spring would be turning to summer in Vermont and he couldn't think of a better way to start his retirement.

The ceiling lights flickered, throwing the whole floor into darkness. The electrics in the design office weren't always the most reliable, especially in the early part of the twentieth century. The building was part of the Chrysler Corporation and had been the home of Antiquarian engineering for the last hundred years. A stasis field had been established around the streamlining division of the famous car manufacturer, one day borrowed from a thousand others, that allowed them to use the facilities of one of the most advanced design departments of its day.

The lights came back on and Henery rubbed his eyes. Switching off the angle-poise lamp, he took his jacket off the back of the chair and picked up his car keys. His wife hadn't been that happy to move back to the twenties, so he'd taken an apartment across town during the week and went back to the lake house at the weekend.

She didn't seem to mind the arrangement; the kids had all flown the nest and she hated it when he came in late and woke her up. Soon it would be over. Once the production was up and running they could take the holiday he'd been promising her for the last two years.

The parking garage was four floors down and Henery liked to take the stairs. He'd never really trusted elevators — not when the electrics were on the fritz, and especially not in the middle of the night when there wasn't anyone around to let him out if they broke down.

Taking the steps two at a time, he reached the basement just as the lights began to flicker again and then went out completely.

'Shit,' Henery said, trying the switch. There was no such thing as emergency lighting back in the twenties. He pulled out his MKIV tachyon and used the torch to find the door.

The garage was like a dark cave, one that reeked of gasoline and tyres, and something else — a rotting smell, like something had crawled into the ventilation and died. He shone the MKIV ahead of him, in the direction of his car. He'd had the same parking space for the last ten years, so there was no problem finding the Airstream C6, even in the dark.

Walking across the asphalt, the smell of decay grew stronger. Henery cursed the failing power for the second time and quickened his stride.

There was a noise from behind him, a deep guttural sound like a wolf. Henery swung the light around the garage, the glow of the tachyon illuminating a tiny sphere around him and making it impossible to see where the sound was coming from.

His mind began to play tricks on him. Was that the sound of claws on the concrete? Or the dripping of a tap somewhere?

Another deep growl confirmed his fears. He waved the light towards it, but there was nothing.

He was only a few metres from the car now, fumbling in his pocket for the keys. The Chrysler Airflow's paintwork gleamed in the light of the tachyon as he ran towards it.

Something caught his foot, sending him crashing onto his knees. Pain shot through his legs as his tachyon and the keys went flying under the car.

Henery could hear the low hiss of the creature's breath as claws wrapped around his ankle and pulled him back into the dark.

15
ATHENÆUM

They arranged to meet in one of the more secluded reading rooms in the Athenaeum, an area of the Library dedicated to the study of the maelstrom.

Lyra was astonished. 'There was no sign of his almanac?'

'None,' replied Sim. 'Someone's stolen it.'

'Protectorate,' Lyra added sternly. 'I bet they've requisitioned it.'

Caitlin looked worried. 'If they've already done that, how long before they come after me?'

'Why would they? They don't know you were there,' Lyra reassured her. 'The continuity principle prohibits them from going back in time without a Copernican warrant and you know how long that could take.'

'Why would they take our copies?' Sim mused, sitting down next to Lyra. 'I would expect the Protectorate to have a whole archive of their own.'

Caitlin had only met the Protectorate once before, on the day her parents had disappeared. She'd been too afraid of the black-masked men and hid behind Rufius as he argued with them about their unannounced arrival.

They were like a police force within the Order, created to stop the unauthorised alteration of the continuum — like jumping back and killing Hitler's grandfather or changing the outcome of the American Civil War. They were a secretive organisation, more like spies than detectives, and they wore masks to hide their identities because they were probably the most hated faction within the Order.

'So, they can't just go back and see what happened?' she asked.

Sim smiled. 'No, that breaks about a hundred sub-clauses of temporal law. Think about it; if they go back and affect the outcome in any way, like, say, trying to prevent it — then it would never have happened and they would never have investigated it. It's basically the Novikov self-consistency principle.'

'And they also don't like putting themselves in danger,' Lyra sneered.

'So, how do we find out what Zillers was caught up in?' Caitlin wondered.

Sim shrugged. 'Go back through his timeline I guess.'

'Isn't that kind of illegal too?'

'Not strictly legal, no, but the Protectorate do it all the time.'

'So where do we start?' asked Caitlin. 'He was nearly eighty — that's a lot of years to work through.'

'We could start in the middle and work outwards?' suggested Sim, moving his hands away from each other.

Caitlin shook her head. 'No, I think we should start by finding out who he really was.'

'Is anyone interested in what I've found out?' Lyra interrupted.

Sim and Caitlin stopped talking and turned towards Lyra. She was glaring at them, tapping her fingers on the open book.

Chimæra

'So, I spoke to my friend in Xeno today and she dismissed the Madrigor as a myth. She's a scientist, so to her these grimoires,' — she held up the book — 'and I quote: "are pure male fantasy depicting self-loathing and debasement of women". Apart from that she was very interested in your creature, though they've not heard anything from the Protectorate about it. She's quite happy to meet up.'

16

OFFICE OF THE PROTECTORATE

[Protectorate HQ. Date: 11.890]

Sabien sat behind his desk staring at the typewritten memo:

TOP SECRET
  FAO: INSP. SABIEN
  CASE: #1829029-1: Arsenius Zillers
  Due to the unnatural nature of the crime protocol 53 has been invoked, requiring the collaboration of the Xenobiology Department. You will extend all courtesy and evidence to their representatives and collaborate in all matters.
  ENDS.
  CHIEF INQUISITOR ECKHART

They've called in the monster squad, Sabien thought to himself. If there was one department he hated more than his own it was the unicorn chasers.

He preferred to work alone. After twenty years in the service, his superiors had eventually grown used to his solitary approach. They couldn't argue with his results — the rest of the murder squad called him 'Sherlock', because no one could solve cases like he could.

When he finally made inspector, his boss had tried to assign him a junior officer, but virtually every one of them had transferred out within three months — except for Maddox.

Halli Maddox was a clever young woman who showed a lot promise. She put up with his short temper and constant griping — calling him cantankerous or 'tank' for short. There had been something about her that was impossible not to like. She had an irrepressible spark, one that no amount of bad shit could seem to put out.

Until she got herself killed.

They had been called in to assist on a particularly horrific series of murders in late Victorian London — someone was killing prostitutes in the East end and the Protectorate officer for that period was failing to contain the situation. Maddox had taken an interest and persuaded Sabien to take the case — against his better judgement.

She was fiercely ambitious, wanting to pass her probation with flying colours — this was exactly the kind of high profile case that would look great on her record and she was impossible to dissuade when she had her mind set on something.

It wasn't obvious at the beginning that it was a monster case; the crimes looked to be more sexually motivated, like the work of a demented saw-bones or butcher.

After countless nights patrolling the murky alleys of

Whitechapel with no sign of a lead, Maddox had suggested she work the case alone for a while. Sabien had other matters that needed his attention and she was quite capable of looking after herself, or so he thought.

There were times when he'd considered going back and saving her. It would finish his career, but no one should end their days in some rat-hole back alley.

The monster turned out to be an organ harvester, called a Xargi. When the Xenos eventually tracked it down they insisted on capturing it alive. The beast put four officers in the hospital and gave Sabien a scar that still bothered him in cold weather.

Sabien screwed up the memo and threw it into the waste bin. Lighting a cigarette, he stared at the unfinished report on the Zillers case sitting in the typewriter.

He'd read the man's dossier and on the surface it appeared that Zillers had been a conscientious member of the Scriptorians. Having worked for most of his life as an archivist, he'd opted for early retirement after the death of his sick wife, taking up a curator role at the Great Library in Alexandria.

But Sabien knew that the documents only told half the story; they didn't capture the little things, his hopes and dreams, the reasons he got up every morning. He had no other family; his wife had died from some kind of cancer and they'd never had kids. He'd hardly made an impact on history with such an uneventful life — which didn't fit with such an unusual death.

He wondered how his own epitaph would read. His career had not progressed well in the Protectorate, despite his natural abilities. He should have been a chief inspector by now, but his maverick nature and general reluctance to kiss ass had limited his rise through the ranks.

He put out the cigarette and started to type. His fingers hesitated over the keys when he reached the 'Witnesses' section of the form. Officially he couldn't mention what he had seen when he'd read the timeline of the staff. Firstly, because it was a breach of protocol: no one was supposed to interrogate the events surrounding a homicide until Copernicans said so, but also because it would mean revealing his ability.

Natural substances like wood were avoided by most members of the Order. They were harder to weave than man-made objects — their chronology was too fragmented; trees captured the passing of time in a fractal, non-linear way, like an ever-changing maze that could trap the user in an eternal loop.

Sabien had read the history of Zillers' staff carefully, not entering the events but merely observing them like a movie, scanning back and forth through the various disconnected moments until he found the owner of the bloody fingerprint — it was a girl, not a monster.

She'd been in the room when Zillers was murdered. Although it was impossible to trace her, the event was so fleeting and the wood gave him little more than a shadow.

He skipped the witness section and moved on to the evidence log.

Suddenly the desk phone rang.

'Inspector Sabien?' asked a woman's voice.

He recognised the dull monotone of the duty officer from the CPD, the Copernican Probability Desk, who monitored the continuum for any unexpected change or deviation of the past.

'Yes.'

'We've intercepted an unforeseen homicide. Its temporal signature has an eighty-four percent correlation with the Zillers incident.'

'When?'

'Temporal coordinates are being synchronised with your almanac now. It occurred in 11.922. Antiquarian by the name of Sergeant, Henery Sergeant — Artificer First Class. But there's a slight problem. The body was discovered thirteen minutes after the murder and the Detroit Police Department are in attendance.'

Thirteen minutes was not a lot to work with, Sabien reflected. He wouldn't be able to get the body moved in time, not without some heavy lifters.

Sabien put down the phone and opened his notebook, watching the details write themselves out onto a blank page.

Time to go native, he thought, walking over to a cabinet and dialling the numbers 11922 into the rotary lock. A range of authentic period suits appeared as the doors slid away.

17

COLONEL RETURNS

Rufius was waiting for Caitlin when she returned to the Chapter House. He was sitting quietly on the back steps shucking raw peas from their pods and eating them.

'Hi,' she greeted him nervously.

His beard had grown a few inches since she'd last seen him; a sure sign that he'd been on a mission, and the military grade-one haircut was a dead giveaway — he'd been off playing soldiers somewhere.

The old man's eyes narrowed slightly. 'Methuselah tells me you've been in a bit of trouble?' There was a hoarseness to his voice, like he'd been shouting.

He stood to let Sim and Lyra pass by. Lyra shot her a look from over Rufius' shoulder, as if to say 'good luck'.

'It was terrible,' said Caitlin, feeling the tears welling up. Rufius was the closest thing she'd had to a father since her parents went missing and he always managed to bring out the child in her.

Over the years he'd taught her so many things; how to survive in some of the bleakest parts of pre-history, how to defend herself against the monsters of the maelstrom, and a hundred other ways to protect herself. She didn't want to admit to him that she'd been so petrified that she couldn't move.

The old man took her in his arms and squeezed her like a giant bear. She buried her face in the layers of his greatcoat and let the tears come flooding out.

No matter how well Lyra had smoothed over the terror of that event, nothing would help her heal like one of his hugs. He made her feel safe, and there wasn't anything that 'Uncle Roofuss' couldn't fix.

'Zillers — the name sounds awfully familiar,' Rufius contemplated, dunking his fourth chocolate bourbon into his tea. The bone china teacup looked ridiculous in his large, rough hands.

They were sitting in the kitchen, one of his favourite places to have a 'proper chat'. A tradition that the two of them had fallen into over the years, it involved copious amounts of tea and an enormous tin of biscuits — preferably from Huntleys.

'He was the curator of maps at the Royal Library, and was helping me with my dissertation on the Mayerstein index.'

Rufius pulled a face. 'Sounds awfully boring.'

'It was,' she said with a sigh. 'I was actually proposing a new approach, but Master Dorrowkind is threatening to fail me.'

'Wouldn't expect anything less.' He nodded. 'So the creature that you saw —'

'The Madrigor,' Caitlin corrected.

Rufius laughed. 'No such thing, bloody Trithemius and his overactive imagination — wasn't a bad cryptographer mind you.' He went to take a fifth bourbon, but changed his mind when he noticed Caitlin glaring at him.

'So, this Madrigor was carving something in Zillers' chest?'

She winced as the memory came flooding back. 'Yes.'

'Did you see what it was? A symbol of some kind?'

Caitlin shook her head.

'Shame. I would bet a sovereign it was some kind of sigil — marking the prey, it would've given a clue to its origination.'

'But why attack him in the first place? He was a quiet, peaceful man who liked maps.'

'Maybe he found something he shouldn't — hard to say without digging into his past.'

'That may be difficult. His records have disappeared.'

'Sequestered by the Protectorate?'

'Lyra thinks so.'

'Do you know who's been assigned to the case?'

She shrugged. 'No idea, but they're going to want to talk to me, aren't they?'

The old man scratched his beard. 'Depends on the investigating officer. They should be more concerned with tracking down the creature — in case it attacks again. Their first priority should be to bring in the Xenos and maybe the Dreadnoughts. If there's been a breach somewhere and this thing is roaming around unchecked — it could get very messy.'

Rufius poured them both a fresh cup of tea.

'So what do I do now?' asked Caitlin.

Rufius scratched his beard and picked up a fig roll. 'Leave it with me. I've got a few favours I can call in, but first we need to sort out your tutor.'

18

FUTURIST

[Belsarus Estate. Date: 11.722]

Johannes Belsarus made the final adjustments to the magnetoscope and stepped back to admire his work. It was the product of a lifetime of experimentation, a masterpiece of temporal engineering. Floating in a lake of mercury, the three brass spheres rotated gyroscopically around each other, generating gravitational fields that created hypnotic ripples across the surface of the liquid metal.

This is going to be my eureka moment, he thought to himself, reviewing the final calculations on his slide rule. The harmonics were tuned to perfection, the oscillating frequencies were within tolerances — nothing could possibly go wrong this time.

For years his peers had mocked him for believing that travel into the future would ever be possible. They'd all abandoned him after the incident at the Royal Society, and his name had become a term of ridicule amongst the academic community — a 'Belsarus Brainstorm' became another word for catastrophe.

Chimæra

'The path of invention is paved with failure,' Belsarus regularly reminded himself as he worked alone. It was one of his favourite sayings, although he could never remember exactly where he'd first heard the phrase.

This was far from his first attempt at a time machine: in fact, this was at least his fortieth. The fortune that his father had left him was completely exhausted and this was probably going to be his last attempt.

Had he been so inclined, he could have counted the exact number of attempts by using the ruined parts of the family estate. The East wing had been entirely destroyed after the fire ten years ago. As a consequence he'd moved his workshop to various outbuildings and barns, but they too were now in rather short supply.

Today's experiment was to take place in the ballroom. The most extravagantly decorated of all the rooms, it too had fallen into disrepair since his mother died. The mirrored walls had all tarnished and the gilding peeled away from the cornices. He remembered how she'd held the most extravagant evenings when he was a child: the entire estate would have been decorated with oriental illuminations and he would be allowed to stay up and watch the guests dance through the long winter nights.

The old grandfather clock chimed the hour. It was midnight — a fitting time for dark deeds, and with every failed experiment his work had become ever darker and more desperate.

The Copernicans were adamant that no one could travel beyond the frontier: the border between the present and the future. No one except the Paradox, of course, who they treated as little more than a statistical anomaly, a rounding error, a fairytale — but not to Belsarus.

He had spent years studying the most archaic books and

treatises on the Paradox. Following the wild imaginings of reavers and seers, searching for clues as to how it could be done, looking for the origins of the prophecy.

There were many systems, both scientific and magical, and he had tried them all.

All except this.

Magnetism, the invisible force of gravity harnessed into a configuration that focused its energy, giving him the power to warp time. The rotating ferrous cores within the spheres created a tempest of magnetic flux that Belsarus had seen affect the very clock that now struck the twelfth bell.

He offered up a silent prayer as he lifted the large diving helmet onto his shoulders, breathing in the iron tang of the air from the compressor as he stepped out of the heavy boots that were weighing him down.

Immediately, he felt the pull of the magnetic force on his body as it lifted him off the ground. Enveloped by waves of energy the world around him began to vibrate — the fabric of reality was being disrupted. His diving helmet was wrenched off his head, and the rivets of his leather suit exploded from their bindings.

Light and dark flashed across the windows as night became day and back again. The rotation of the magnetoscope increased, the spinning spheres becoming a blur, glowing with an intensity of a star. The room disappeared, darkness folding in around him as time stilled and a thousand different eventualities expanded before his eyes.

This was the frontier, the nexus between present and the many potential futures. He could feel the millions of possibilities flowing through his body, weaving into a single moment, and there beyond it all, was the undiscovered country.

As he floated at the border of tomorrow, he wept — knowing that this was as far as he would ever go. The past bound him to the present like an anchor chain, and he felt every part of his life pulling him back.

The high-pitched whine of gears grinding against each other broke through his reverie. Belsarus watched the myriad strands of destiny fade away as his machine powered down. The walls of his house solidified, the floor returning beneath his feet.

Collapsing to his knees he took a deep breath, the first he'd taken in what seemed like an eternity. He was naked, and steam rose off his sweat drenched skin.

The clock was still striking the hour.

The realisation of what he'd witnessed overwhelmed him, and he broke down, frustration and despair manifesting in a long mournful wail — he had seen the future, but he could never travel to it.

As Belsarus knelt in the darkened ruins he caught his reflection in one of the grand mirrors. The image shimmered slightly, as though the surface were vibrating. Looking around him he saw that it wasn't the ballroom that he'd left, but a more decrepit version, tarnished and aged.

He began to laugh. All this time and he'd been looking in the wrong place.

19

THE MORGUE

[Autopsy, Detroit. Date: 11.930]

Inspector Sabien studied the body as it lay on the marble slab, the pale white flesh in sharp contrast to the bright red wounds that were carved into his chest. They were deep rents; the flesh had been sliced through to the bone, but there was no blood — it had been done post-mortem.

As with Zillers, the slashes appeared to form a rudimentary symbol. Sabien consulted his almanac and compared this version with the sketch he'd made of the first victim. They were different, so he copied it down, carefully noting the changes and attaching a request for a Scriptorian search with any known alphabet.

On the inside of his arm was a series of Roman numerals.

III-VI-MXII

'What's the significance of the numbers?' he asked the pathologist.

'Don't know, could be a date?'

Earlier, when Sabien had arrived at the crime scene, the garage was already crawling with Dreadnoughts and Protectorate officers mingling with the local police force. They blended in seamlessly with the linears; their uniforms and mid-western accents were perfect.

Some over-eager Copernican at CPD had obviously escalated the status of the incident, deciding that two similar events in less than forty-eight hours constituted a major emergency, and called in every department she could think of.

Dreadnought lensmen were busy pretending to photograph the area while scanning for breaches, while the local police were drinking coffee and watching a tracker dog go under cars and into dark corners.

It was mayhem. No one was coordinating — any forensic evidence would've been contaminated and worse than useless. His chance to observe and absorb the details of the death had been lost.

When Sabien learned that the Detroit Police had already moved the body, he knew there was little reason to stay. Since it was the 11.930s, at least there would be photographs, but pictures would be useless for a physical trace, and when the rest of his team arrived looking like something from the Untouchables, Sabien took it as his cue to leave and went to the mortuary.

'Time of death?' asked Sabien.

'Early hours of this morning. The lower temperatures in the garage might have slowed the process a little,' the pathologist observed from behind a surgical mask, probing the lacerations with a pair of forceps.

Sabien leaned in to get a closer look at the cuts. 'Would you say there was a pattern to those wounds?'

'Not that I've noticed. Although they weren't the cause of death. There's some serious trauma to the cranium — see the bruising on both sides of the skull?'

Sabien moved around the table to look at the victim's face. The eyes were wild and staring, and a grimace distorted the features where rigor mortis had set in. The doctor was right; each temple was bruised in the shape of a thumb.

'The man's head has been crushed by a very powerful pair of hands,' added the pathologist. 'And there's also this.' He pulled a long, crystalline claw out of one of the cuts and dropped it into a metal dish.

Sabien picked it up with a gloved hand. It was translucent, like glass, and curved in a crescent shape with serrations along the inner edge that would make a perfect ripping tool for opening up a body.

'Some kind of big cat maybe?' the doctor wondered, staring at the claw.

Sabien shrugged. 'Too early to say, but I'll get it over to forensics,' he lied, putting the claw into a small jar and watching as it left a bloody smear down the side of the glass.

The pathologist picked up a vicious looking saw. 'I'm going to open him up now. Are you staying or have you seen enough?'

Sabien pocketed the jar and turned to leave, then remembered something. 'What happened to his clothes?'

'They've already gone to the lab. Johnson would be the man to ask.'

20
MEETING

Dorrowkind sat opposite Rufius and Caitlin, his eyes nervously flicking from one to the other. She enjoyed the way he was agitated by her guardian's presence. Rufius tended to have that affect on people, especially pompous overweight masters with an air of undeserved superiority.

'Your ward has been rather challenging this term,' Dorrowkind complained. 'I hardly see how extending the deadline over the summer holidays would improve her chances of attaining a pass.'

Rufius sighed deeply and glanced over at her. He'd been in more than one meeting like this over the years, and every time she'd promised him it would be the last. Yet here they were again. She could tell from his expression that she was on thin ice.

'Master Dorrowkind, there are extenuating circumstances that will prevent her from completing the work. She's been seconded by the Watch to assist on a highly sensitive mission.'

Dorrowkind sneered at the name of the Watch, but Rufius had grown used to it — his group were barely tolerated by the other guilds. They were mavericks, misfits who'd been cast out and found themselves recruited into what most saw as the worst job in the Order.

It was the role of the Watchmen to carry out the 'adjustments', or 'repairs', as Rufius preferred to call them. They were the ones in the field, getting their hands dirty, the agents of change who saw first hand the impact of the Order's theoretical improvements.

Dorrowkind scoffed. 'I have already extended the deadline by a week. I'm sure the Watch is perfectly capable of operating without the assistance of one student.'

Caitlin saw the fury building in Rufius' cheeks; he wasn't a man that suffered fools, nor did he have a great affinity for 'armchair academics'.

'This is not a request,' Rufius growled, raising himself to his full height and towering over the trembling tutor. 'You will extend every courtesy to her and I will personally ensure that the work is completed by next semester. You have my word.'

Dorrowkind knew better than to question his honour. Before he could respond, Rufius was heading for the door. Caitlin bowed slightly to the master and hurried after him.

'Don't think that went too well,' Rufius mumbled as he marched along the corridor.

'At least you didn't punch this one,' Caitlin said, and chuckled.

'True.'

'So what's next?'

'You're going to finish your damned homework and I'm going to see Alixia about a favour.'

21

FORENSICS

[Protectorate HQ. Date: 11.890]

Sabien went back over his case notes. So far he had very little to go on — the two victims were only connected by their murderer. There was nothing in their records that linked them in any way.

Zillers had worked in records and Sergeant was some golden boy of Antiquarian engineering. Neither had any history of arcane practices; no reaving, no rituals and definitely no association with any known criminals. Both of them seemed to be perfectly ordinary members of the Order, something which always made Sabien suspicious — nobody was ever that perfect.

As investigations go this wasn't turning out to be one of his best, and his case load was stacking up on the desk: the pile of manila folders was increasing by at least an inch every time he came back into the office.

There were a hundred other things he should have been doing and he knew that he was devoting far too much time to this one, but it bothered him — he hated spooky shit like this; it reminded him too much of Maddox, and maybe that was the problem.

Johnson in forensics was one of their own, a boring little Antiquarian who, from his sour expression, Sabien could tell wasn't a big fan of the Protectorate.

He'd got used to that a long time ago. Nobody liked a police force, especially one that could go back and check your alibi. It didn't help that most of his colleagues preferred to mask their identities and work in the shadows. Sabien didn't go in for all that cloak and dagger stuff. He refused to wear the mask, preferring to question his suspects face to face.

'Did you find any other fibres on his clothes?'

Johnson had Sergeant's suit carefully laid out on the table. He wore a large lens array on a leather helmet strapped to his head.

'Do you know how many other contaminants we come into contact with in our daily lives?'

'Okay. So let's narrow it down. Human hair, specifically female.'

Johnson smirked. 'Looking for a femme fatale?'

'Do you know how many murders are committed by people known to the victim?'

Johnson consulted his notes. 'There were a number of strands, yes. But they all matched those of his wife, sorry.'

Sabien considered whether to show him the claw, but there was something obnoxious about the look on the man's face that made him hold back.

'Have the clackers decided how they're going to keep this out of the papers?'

Clackers was another name for the Copernicans; their

computers were all mechanical and made a hell of a racket when in full swing.

'I'm sure they'll find a local perp to blame this on,' Sabien replied, turning to leave.

'There's always the Black Legion. You can pretty much hang any one of them and no one would bat an eyelid.'

Sabien had heard of the Legion, a Klan-like group that had risen out of southeast Michigan. It wouldn't be the first time the Copernicans used a scapegoat.

'I heard its another ripper case,' Johnson said, opening the suit and inspecting the dark blood stain on the lining.

'Too early to say,' Sabien said dismissively. 'Send me the report as soon as you're done.'

Flicking through the pages of his almanac, Sabien looked over the notes on the hard evidence: the claw and the markings on the victim's chests. He knew instinctively that the symbols meant something, but hadn't heard anything back from the Scriptorians — which was no surprise, though it meant he would to have to find his own specialist in oriental languages.

And at some point he was going to have to talk to the monster squad about the claw, but that could wait too. First he wanted to track down the witness.

A junior officer knocked on the door frame.

'S-Sir?'

There was an unwritten rule within the department that no one disturbed Sabien while he was working — especially when he was reviewing his case notes. They'd obviously sent the new boy, Jamieson, as some kind of initiation.

'You'd better have a real good reason to be here constable Jamieson,' Sabien growled without looking up from his desk.

'They've f-found another body.'

[New York Date: 11.876]

Her body was contorted, its arms and legs bent at impossible angles. When Sabien touched her skin, it was like ice. He'd learned that body temperature reduced at one-and-a-half degrees per hour after death, meaning that this poor woman had been dead for longer than any of the others.

The scenes-of-crime crew had just arrived and were busy documenting the various artefacts. Her penthouse apartment was a shrine to the occult, full of ritualistic artefacts and manuscripts that looked like a reavers wet dream.

Except this victim was not a member of the Order. She was a linear, travelling forward through time at the normal rate, one second per second.

The bruising around her temples matched the other two victims, and the lacerations on her chest were as cryptic as before.

This makes it a serial case, Sabien thought to himself. *Now the carnival begins.*

She had died in front of a large black mirror, on which the silvering had perished and there was a large jagged crack running from a hole in the upper right corner. A book lay open on the floor in front of the mirror. Its pages were soaked in her blood and it was impossible to make out what she'd been reading when she was attacked. Checking that no one was watching, he touched an unspoilt part of the vellum and felt the history unravel — then wished he hadn't.

The book had once belonged to Belsarus, the crazy Antiquarian inventor who had tried to travel into the future.

'Should we move her?' asked Jamieson, standing beside the body. 'Or leave the stasis field in place?'

'Leave it,' Sabien ordered, putting his gloves back on. 'We can't touch anything until the Dreadnoughts have done a lens sweep.'

He had no excuse for ignoring protocol 53 now. They would have to bring in the unicorn chasers.

22

XENOBIOLOGY

[Royal Zoological Gardens, London. Date: 11.828]

The Xenobiology department was located beneath the Royal Zoological Gardens in Regent's Park. Hidden in a sub-basement a hundred feet below, it was one of the most difficult departments to gain access to — mainly because it was one of the most dangerous.

There were many rumours about the xenobiologysts that worked there; how they'd lost limbs and even lives to the creatures they studied, and how they ensnared the monsters of the maelstrom using themselves as bait, and other crazy stories.

Sim's mother, Alixia, was affiliated to the Xenos. As an 'Extinction Curator', she had dedicated her life to cultivating and studying extinct species, some of which she insisted on keeping around the house. Her Dodo, Maximillian, had a voracious appetite for fish, and was highly entertaining when he managed to get into the kitchen. Whereas, nobody dare go down to the baths in the basement during the times when Alixia was working on the plesiosaur mating project.

The Xenos were closely allied to the Draconian guild as their studies centred on the nightmarish creatures that spawned from the maelstrom — a place outside of the timestream and the nearest thing Caitlin could imagine to hell.

The creatures that broke through the chronosphere were pure evil. Caitlin had only encountered a few: Monads, which were a kind of memory vampire, and Strzyga who were demons that absorbed their victim's timelines. The Xenos had found hundreds more.

Some members of the Order believed there were a host of primeaval gods, known as 'the elders', and who were thought to hold dominion over the chaotic realm.

She had her own reasons for hating the maelstrom. It cast a dark shadow in her heart where her parents should have been. They had been lost while defending one of the worst breaches in the Order's history. Hundreds of Draconians had died that day, most of them sucked into the maelstrom, never to be seen again. She couldn't think about them without imagining what terrors they must have encountered in there.

The entrance to the Xeno department was hidden halfway down the East Tunnel. Caitlin and Lyra followed Rufius and Alixia through a nondescript metal door that led to a cast-iron spiral staircase. As they descended, the smell reminded her of a pond after it had been drained. She tried not to breathe through her nose while staying close behind Rufius.

His Russian army boots clanged on the metal steps like hammer blows as he took them two at a time. Alixia, on the other hand, seemed to float like a prima-ballerina, as though her feet weren't actually touching the floor. She was the epitome of a lady, polite and well-mannered, but also so incredibly intelligent and strong-willed, and Caitlin loved her deeply.

It struck her at that moment that these were the two most important people in her life — the ones that had cared for her for the last seven years. She smiled, trying to imagine a more diverse set of role models than a soldier and a princess.

Rufius hadn't been keen to bring Caitlin to the Xeno department, but Alixia insisted.

She had returned the previous evening from an expedition in the Mesolithic and the discussion over dinner that night had descended into the usual battle of stubbornness and gentle persuasion, which Caitlin had learned to excuse herself from a long time ago. Although on this occasion she decided to sit on the stairs and listen.

'Dangerfield is one of the most dedicated xenobiologysts I have ever met,' Alixia declared in her calm but forthright way. 'I am sure he would be more than happy to help us identify the creature.'

'But the place is not safe! You know what happened the last time I went down there.'

Alixia scoffed. 'It was your own stupid fault! Everyone knows you don't touch an Oxylotal with your bare hands.'

'And she's got coursework to finish!'

'Well, that's rich coming from you! How many times did you pull her out of school to go on one of your crazy adventures?'

'A couple?' Rufius sounded sheepish.

'Three times a year for five years. Not including that little sojourn into the temple of inscriptions in Palenque. I've spent more time in the headmaster's office apologising about her absences than I ever did with the others. You're a terrible influence on her!'

Methuselah, who had been quietly drinking throughout their argument, poured them both a large glass of wine. 'Now let's not drag up the past. She's had the best of both of you, so there's no doubt she will succeed in whatever she chooses to do.'

They ignored him, but his calm interruption seemed to dissipate the tension.

'You can try and persuade Master Dorrowkind not to fail her then,' growled Rufius.

'Fine,' Alixia's snapped. 'I've become quite the expert at it.'

The door to the Xeno department was like something from a bank vault. It was constructed from a set of heavy, circular brass discs with locking bolts every thirty degrees. In the centre was a series of concentric circles, similar to those on a tachyon, except these rings were engraved with symbols of different sets of animals.

Alixia stepped up to the door and rotated the dials, unlocking all of the bolts in sequence as she carefully aligned each of the twelve combinations.

Caitlin felt a little nervous as the final lock sprang open. She tried not to think about the creature that killed Zillers, but the idea that it might be behind this door — that somehow they'd caught it and she would have to face it again — made her feel sick.

The mechanism's gears ground into action and the door retreated away to reveal a shimmering wall of light.

'Temporal shielding,' whispered Lyra, who had insisted on coming along once she heard Caitlin was going. 'The whole department is contained within a stasis field.'

Rufius followed Alixia through the rippling mirror wall, Lyra and Caitlin following close behind.

The central laboratory was housed in an enormous circular fortress. Curved iron stairs wound around and up the inside of the metal walls, leading to platforms with sets of riveted pressure doors — the kind they used on submarines.

Men and women in heavily shielded suits clumped up and down between the floors carrying large specimen jars and lethal looking instruments — the whole scene looked more like something from a nuclear power station than a biology department.

A small group of scientists gathered around Alixia the moment she arrived. They had removed their headgear and were busy chatting to her like old friends.

Rufius grew bored of waiting for Alixia to finish the pleasantries and went to watch a team decanting an unusual specimen from one of the tall glass containers that hung above their heads.

'Wow, can you feel it?' asked Lyra, waving her hands in mystical patterns in front of her.

'What?' asked Caitlin, looking around the laboratory.

'The emanations. They're totally off the scale.'

Caitlin had no idea what Lyra was sensing. She'd never been even vaguely empathic, one of the skills that made her adopted sister such a talented seer.

'No.'

'God, it must be weird to be so shut-off, so disconnected from everything.'

Caitlin knew her too well to take offence. Lyra had a knack for bluntness — she was a savant, a high-functioning autistic, and there wasn't a filter for what came out of her mouth.

'What can you feel?'

'Hmm? Mostly bat-shit crazy stuff. Broken record kind of

insanity,' she mumbled, wandering over to one of the glass chambers that was full of luminous green gas. 'Some of these babies have been in here for centuries. They've forgotten what they were.'

A tentacle unfurled against the inner side of the glass, followed by something that could have been a head or its arse — it was hard to tell.

Caitlin pulled Lyra back from the chamber. 'Probably best if you don't get too close. You're too sensitive to deal with their pain.'

They watched Rufius trying to help the team decanting the small, albino whale from the glass. Caitlin could tell his assistance wasn't appreciated.

'He's such a lump.' Lyra said, giggling. 'They're going to drop it if they're not careful.'

'Is your friend here?' wondered Caitlin, trying not to laugh as Rufius pulled the wrong chain and sent the team into a frenzy of activity.

Lyra shook her head. 'No, she works over in research, at the Natural History Museum.'

Alixia returned with an Asian woman in a grey flight suit, a large cat walking beside her.

'Girls, I would like to introduce Kaori Shika.'

Kaori performed a formal oriental bow while her cat sat and cleaned itself.

'And this is Schrödinger. A Xenosmilus — one of the Machairodontinae Sabre-tooths.' Kaori explained.

'This is Caitlin, and my daughter Lyra. They are very interested in your department, and as I have some business with Doctor Dangerfield I wondered if you would be so kind as to show them around?'

Alixia walked off, leaving them alone with Kaori. Lyra went over to stroke the sabre-tooth.

'I wouldn't,' Kaori warned. It began to nuzzle against Lyra's hand. 'He doesn't usually do that,' the scientist added, looking rather bemused.

'Lyra's a seer,' Caitlin explained. 'She's probably imprinted herself on his subconscious.'

'Ah, that makes sense.'

'I've just decanted a Qalupalik,' gushed Rufius, rejoining them.

He bowed to Kaori and greeted her in fluent Japanese. Caitlin could tell she was impressed, although she had no idea when he'd been sent to Japan.

'So what would you like to see first?' she asked, waving her arm around the laboratory.

'I heard a rumour you have a Firedrake?' said Rufius eagerly, like a child in a sweet shop.

Kaori smiled awkwardly. 'A time dragon? Of course, they're right next to the unicorns on the second floor.'

The old man looked a little disappointed.

Kaori smiled. 'Let's start with the basic xenoforms shall we?' She took his arm and guided him up the staircase. 'We use four classifications: corporeal, non-corporeal, linear and non-linear, and we keep them on separate floors for obvious reasons.'

Caitlin and Lyra waited for the sabre-tooth to follow his mistress and fell in line behind them.

23
CASE MEETING

[Protectorate HQ. Date: 11.890]

'There have been three murders so far,' Sabien began reluctantly, pointing to the case notes projected onto the screen.

The darkened office was filled with the other members of the homicide department, a motley crew of grizzled old lifers and baby-faced juniors. It was well known that few chose to remain in homicide after their first rotation, and those that did were not staying there out of choice.

Sabien hated briefings, but protocol dictated that once there were three similar deaths it became a serial case, and that meant putting the whole team on it.

'A retired Scriptorian by the name of Zillers was the first to be discovered, but not the first to die. According to time-of-death from forensics, that was a linear by the name of Delawney, a sixty-year-old heiress with a penchant for arcane rituals.'

He consciously neglected to mention Belsarus' book; just the mention of his name would turn the meeting into a farce.

'Victim number three was an Antiquarian called Sergeant. All had the same MO: skulls crushed with extreme force, and some kind of symbol carved into their chest.'

He nodded to the projectionist, who slid a photographic plate of Sergeant's autopsy into the magic lantern. Everyone leaned forwards to get a better look at the macabre details.

'Each of the symbols appear to be taken from a separate archaic language and they were all made post-mortem by an extremely sharp blade that cut so deep it scored the breast bone. So far there's no real motive, nor anything to link the victims other than the way they died. Questions?'

One of the juniors held up his hand. 'Are the monster squad involved?'

'Yes,' Sabien said through a grimace, 'but we're not treating this as a Xeno case, not yet anyway.'

His boss, Chief Inspector Joseph Avery, who'd been leaning against the back wall, uncrossed his arms and walked towards the front.

'Thank you inspector,' he said, nodding to Sabien. 'This has all the hallmarks of a storm-kin attack, so you all know the procedure: we have a duty to inform the other guilds as soon as possible. Mayberry, you're in charge of comms, so prepare a bulletin and get the Copernicans to push it out in the next hour. Davies, choose two constables and get your arses down to records and pull everything on Zillers and Sergeant. Hartz, you're on your own I'm afraid. Go and find out about the linear Delawney.'

Avery took Sabien to one side as the others left. 'Michael, I know the Xenos aren't your favourite department, and personally I can't blame you after that fiasco with Maddox, but since you're SIO on this you'll have to suck it up. I suggest you arrange a meeting with their coordinator ASAP.'

24

GYNÆPHORA

The hall of corporeal exhibits was a museum of the most horrific specimens Caitlin had ever seen. Preserved in giant glass tubes filled with sickly yellow liquid were the slowly decaying remains of Monads, Strzyga, Revenants and many different species she couldn't identify.

A group of xenobiologists were gathered around a large marble dissection table in the centre of the hall. The flaccid corpse of a large creature was spread out across it, the skin of its chest pinned back to reveal the internal organs.

'Anatomy class,' Kaori explained. 'Looks like they've caught themselves a Crysotrix. Want to see?'

The others nodded and followed.

'The Crysotrix has five primary hearts and two secondaries,' instructed the tutor, pointing to a series of pallid organs. 'We believe the creature uses as many as three during mating and all seven in combat. The configuration of the male's skull spines match exactly with the positions of the primaries, ensuring that one strike to an opponent's chest could puncture all of the coronary vessels and completely incapacitate their foe.'

Kaori and the others stood behind the students, while Rufius stepped through to take a closer look.

'Met one of these bastards once — likes to go for the eyes.'

The teacher scowled at the interruption. 'As I was about to say, one of the key points to note is their love of the vitreous humour, the gel found in the human eye.'

'When are we going to ask her about the Madrigor?' Lyra whispered to Caitlin.

'When he stops making an arse of himself,' Caitlin replied, nodding towards Rufius, who was telling the group about how he killed two Crysotrix with his bare hands.

Kaori and the others seemed to be enjoying his story, but their teacher was not so impressed and began to dissect one of its four lungs.

'I wouldn't do that if I were you,' warned Rufius, catching the man's hand.

'Why an earth not?' His blade hovered over the putrid yellow sac.

'They've terrible breath when they're alive. I've a feeling it's even worse after death.'

'Poppycock,' protested the tutor, wrenching his hand free.

The steel blade sank into the slimy surface of the lung and the tissue parted as he sliced it vertically along the superior lobe.

A faint green gas issued from the incision and the effect of the smell was instantaneous — two of the students immediately threw up on their boots. The others ran away coughing and retching.

Caitlin and Lyra had covered their mouths and noses at Rufius' warning and were spared the worst of it.

Kaori had turned grey, but managed to save her dignity, unlike the tutor who was barfing into a specimen tray.

It took all the way to the end of the corporeal section for the old man to stop laughing.

'So, where would you like to go next?' asked Kaori. 'Would you like to see some ghosts? We have a very interesting collection.'

The hall of the non-corporeal was a very different experience to its counterpart. It was extremely cold, like a deep freeze, and Kaori made them put on thick, heated parkas before they went in.

'We've found that we can contain them in freezing conditions. Minus two hundred and seventy-three degrees, or zero Kelvins. It slows their molecular structures enough for us to see them.'

The creatures were like the most beautifully delicate ice sculptures. Trapped behind frosted glass windows was the most extraordinary display of beasts Caitlin had ever seen. Which was kind of ironic, since in their native state, none of them were visible.

'Doctor Dangerfield perfected the process himself. He was the first biologyst to capture a nethershark.' She waved her mitten towards the giant shark-like beast that hung in the air above their heads.

'Are they all from the maelstrom?' asked Caitlin, staring at a dragon-headed snake.

Kaori nodded. 'Every one. The laws of time aren't the only thing that doesn't seem to apply beyond the chronosphere. We think that some of these may share basic morphology with their linear ancestors, but since they've had an eternity to evolve its virtually impossible to trace their predecessors.'

'How exactly do you go about catching something you can't see?' Rufius asked.

His beard was turning white as his breath crystallised on it, and his nose had gone bright red. Caitlin thought he was turning into a scruffy version of Santa Claus.

Kaori blew out a stream of air in an arc around her. Tiny moth-like creatures were caught in the ice crystals that formed, the weight on their wings causing them to drop to the floor.

'Gynaephora, a harmless non-corp. We believe it is distantly related to the arctic moth.'

Rufius and the others laughed as they all blew streams of smoke out and a hundred moths froze in space. The idea that creatures were moving unseen through the same space as them disturbed Caitlin. It was the same when she used to go swimming in the sea; she hated the idea that there were things under her she couldn't see.

'So, Schrödinger and I have work to do,' said Kaori, pulling off her mittens and stamping the snow off her boots. 'Is there anything else you'd like to know?'

'Have you ever —' Lyra began.

'We had a question about a non-linear,' Caitlin interrupted, before Lyra had time to use the word 'Madrigor'.

'Fire away. Non-Lins are my specialty.'

Caitlin paused, trying to think of the right way to phrase it. 'I saw something the other day. It looked like it had been burned, and there were no eyes or nose, but teeth — lots of teeth, and claws that looked like crystal.'

Kaori looked puzzled. 'Not something I've come across. Where exactly did you see this creature?'

'The library of Alexandria.'

'And what was it doing in the Royal Library?'

Rufius stepped in front of Caitlin protectively. 'Killing one of the curators.'

Kaori's eyes went wide. 'Really? You witnessed the attack?'

Caitlin nodded.

'And did you see how it got there?' Kaori asked, taking out her almanac.

'No.'

'And it didn't touch you?'

Caitlin shook her head.

Kaori could see she was getting upset. 'Sorry, I forget what it's like for non-Xenos. So do you think you could show me where it happened?'

25

BIGELOW

Access to the Xeno laboratory was restricted — because their work was thought to be too dangerous, so they kept an office at the Museum of Natural History in 11.888, for administration and research.

As Sabien walked down the corridor towards the liaison desk he tried to remember what Maddox used to say about them.

She had never understood why he disliked the monster squad. She was fascinated by them, calling his misgivings nothing more than an 'irrational fear of the unknown', a phrase she'd picked up in one of her psychology evening classes.

He'd made some flippant remark about them believing in fairies and she'd got mad and given him a lecture on how important it was to understand everything about the maelstrom and not walk around with his head up his arse trying to pretend the monsters didn't exist.

The Xeno team that had turned up that night in the East

End were led by an American called James Bigelow. He was a big man with a long claw scar down his face which went through his lip, making it curl up in a permanent half-smile. He wore a long leather coat, and a hat that made him look like a cattle rancher.

Bigelow acted like someone who'd seen it all before. While Maddox explained about the traces they had found on the victims, he looked disinterested — treating them like they were amateurs.

Two days later Maddox was dead and Sabien was in the hospital — but Bigelow got his monster.

And now, ten years later he was going to have to work with him again.

When Sabien discovered that Bigelow was working at the liaison desk, he assumed that it was because he'd finally pissed someone off enough to get demoted.

What he wasn't expecting was for it to be on medical grounds.

The man he met when he walked into the office was nothing like the arrogant cowboy of the past.

'I know what you're thinking,' said Bigelow, using the claw of his prosthetic arm to hold out a cigarette.

Sabien took one and sat down. The man had grown fat, and what was left of his hair was cut short. There were many more scars, and under his shirt Sabien could see his right arm was constructed of metal and wires.

'Got into a bad situation with a Qinotaur, back in the tenth. Took the medics two days to put me back together. Couldn't save my arm, or my legs.' He pushed back from the desk and showed off the wheelchair.

Sabien felt all the anger he'd stored up melt away. Bigelow had paid a heavy price in the line of duty. He still hated what had happened to Maddox, but now all he had was pity for the man.

'Guess you're here about a protocol fifty-three?' he asked, taking out a pink form from a drawer.

Sabien nodded and lit his cigarette. 'Orders from the Chief Inquisitor herself.'

'My, we are honoured!' the American said sarcastically.

Sabien took out the case notes and went to hand them over. Bigelow waved his claw at the in-tray. 'Stick 'em on the pile. I'll read them later. Rather you told me about this one in person. Considering how you left us out of the loop for so long.'

Sabien gave him the run down on the three murders, again leaving out the part about Belsarus, the claw and the witness. They were his best leads and he wasn't about to hand them over.

'Sounds like one for Dr Shika,' said Bigelow when Sabien had finished. 'She's one of the best unicorn chasers we have.'

They both smiled.

Bigelow opened up his almanac with his good hand. 'I'll drop her a note. Get her to meet you at the first crime scene.'

Sabien stood up and made to leave.

'Tell me, off the record, you planning to go back and save Maddox one day?' he asked.

Sabien turned back towards Bigelow and nodded.

'Be careful, man,' the American said, holding up his metal hand. 'That Xargi ain't going to play nice.'

26

LIBRARY

[Great Library of Alexandria, Egypt. Date: 9.780]

Sabien decided to go back to the day before the murder. He wanted to see what the place was like before it got ransacked. It was a breach of protocol, but since the case was getting nowhere and the body count was growing he decided it was okay to break a few rules.

On the upper floors of the Library the air was humid and stuffy. The desert winds made no real impact on the temperature, and he began to wish he'd changed out of the standard issue uniform.

He hadn't attempted to blend in. The suit was designed to travel back over ten millennia, so it looked relatively unusual, but no more so than a Roman Legionnaire or a Syrian Trader. Alexandria was a metropolitan capital and the locals were used to some extremely diverse cultures.

He spotted Zillers walking through the main atrium. The old man leaned heavily on the staff as he slowly shuffled through the crowd of academics. Sabien kept a safe distance as he followed him down the stairs into the cooler basement.

There was no sign of the woman; in fact there were hardly any women within the building at all. These were very different times. He'd once had a long discussion with Maddox about the difficulty female officers faced going back into the past — the roles they could adopt were limited once you got back past the nineteenth century.

Sabien waited a few minutes before entering the map chamber. He had to be careful not to accidentally bump into Zillers and change some part of his daily routine.

The old curator was off in one of the alcoves, humming to himself as he sorted through his plans chests. Sabien had a photographic memory, and as he scanned the room he compared it with the image of the crime scene. The cloak was in its proper place, and he noted the staff next to it, where he'd assumed it should have been tomorrow. Other than the floor being clear of charts, nothing else seemed to be out-of-place, except for one thing.

There was a mirror on one wall, a polished bronze disc surrounded by carvings of sea creatures.

It was nothing more than a piece of vanity, a treasure from an Egyptian princess, but what struck Sabien was that in his remembering of the crime scene he saw it as a dull metal shield. There was nothing left of the highly polished surface.

'Can I help you?' asked Zillers, coming out of the alcove. He looked a little surprised.

'I was looking for Seneca,' Sabien said, trying to sound lost.

Zillers smiled. 'Elder or Younger?'

'Younger.'

'Wrong century. You're about two hundred years south of where you need to be. Follow the Caesars up to Nero, and you'll find his works on the twelfth I believe.'

Sabien nodded his thanks and shifted forward twenty-four hours — just after the murder.

The mirror was no longer shining, and its surface was tarnished. He heard voices approaching and stepped back into the shadows.

The map room was exactly as Caitlin remembered, except for the body — there was just a dark stain where Zillers had been.

Rufius and Lyra left her alone, making their excuses and pottering around the archives pretending to look at random charts.

Kaori however, was more direct. 'Did you see where it came from?' she asked, watching her cat as it explored the alcove and sniffed at the blood stains on the flagstones.

'No,' Caitlin answered, trying really hard not to visualise the scene. 'It had already dragged him in there when I came in.'

'And it was bipedal? Like a man — walking on two legs?'

'Kind of, it was on all fours when I saw it, but it looked human — like it used to be a man.'

Caitlin watched in disbelief as the Cat's large pink tongue unfurled and licked the floor.

'Don't let him do that!' she cried.

'How else would he find a trail?' Kaori asked, kneeling beside him.

'I don't know, can't he just sniff Zillers' cloak or something?'

'It's hardly going to contain any data from the creature is it?

'No. But that's just wrong.'

'Do you want to find this thing or not?' Kaori snapped,

standing up. Her eyes were like two chips of flint and Caitlin realised that she was at the end of her tether.

'I just don't think it's very respectful.'

Kaori tutted, taking out her almanac. 'I don't think the creature that attacked him was that respectful either.'

Her eyes narrowed as she read a message. 'Shit,' she said under her breath and scribbled a quick response.

The cat continued to sniff and taste the floor, following a route back towards the chart table.

'He's got a scent, so we need to move — be ready when he jumps out.'

'Your cat can weave?' Caitlin said in disbelief.

Kaori smiled like a proud parent at a prize-giving. 'Since he was three months old. We called him "Schrödinger" after the experiment.'

'What experiment?'

'Schrödinger's cat was a thought experiment devised by Erwin Schrödinger in 11.935 to describe the paradox of quantum superposition,' a man's voice interrupted from the shadows.

Kaori's cat hissed and the hackles rose along the fur on his back.

'Inspector, how nice of you to join us,' Kaori said, patting her cat's head.

A tall, dark-haired man stepped into the light. Caitlin noticed the Protectorate insignia immediately; every officer had their badge and number tattooed onto their neck.

'Sabien,' he said as a way of introduction, his keen brown eyes never leaving Caitlin for a moment.

'You appear to have neglected to report this particular incident to us.'

He shrugged. 'I've been busy.'

'You know the protocol on creature attacks.'

'I know the law,' he said, walking towards Caitlin, 'especially pertaining to fleeing the scene of a crime.'

Caitlin shrank back a little.

'I was told you were coming to share information with us,' Kaori protested, 'not to apprehend the only witness.'

Rufius came storming out from the archives. 'You keep your damned hands off her! She's not a suspect.'

Sabien's hand pulled back his long coat to reveal a lethal-looking samurai sword. 'This is official business, Watchman. I suggest you step back.'

Caitlin shook her head at the old man; this wasn't his fight. His fists clenched as he wrestled with the urge to punch the inspector.

Sabien took out his almanac. 'Name?'

'Caitlin. Caitlin Makepiece.'

'Makepiece,' he repeated as he wrote. 'Guild?'

She bit her lip, forcing out the words when he looked up from the page. 'Scriptorian — Acolyte.'

Schrödinger hissed at him.

Sabien turned to Kaori. 'If you cannot control that animal I'll have it put down.'

Kaori glared at him and stroked her cat's head.

Sabien took out a pair of handcuffs. 'Caitlin Makepiece, I'm charging you with perverting the course of justice. Your rights and privileges as a member of the Order are hereby suspended.'

In one fluid motion he snapped the shackles onto her wrists and pulled out his sword, pointing it directly at Rufius whose cheeks were burning red.

'Last warning, old man.'

A second later Caitlin and the inspector disappeared.

'They can't do that!' Lyra cried.

Kaori shook her head in disbelief. 'Oh they can, and they

do. The Protectorate is full of arrogant pricks like him who think they can just turn up and threaten people's cats.'

'What are we going to do?' asked Lyra, turning to Rufius.

But the old man had gone.

Schrödinger roared as he wound around his mistress.

'He's re-acquired the scent,' Kaori said, grabbing the cat's collar. 'Sorry, I've got to go.'

Lyra shrugged and waved them both goodbye.

She was all alone in the dark, eerie basement. A shiver crept down her spine as she hugged herself and looked around the room.

'Now what would Caitlin do next?' she asked herself, trying to be brave.

Suddenly, Kaori reappeared. 'You're going to want to see this!' she said, holding out her hand.

Lyra smiled and took it.

27
INTERVIEW

[Protectorate HQ. Date: Classified]

The room was a grey, featureless box.

Caitlin had always imagined that the Protectorate interrogated their prisoners in medieval torture chambers, with braziers full of glowing metal instruments and things for pulling out teeth.

There was a table and two chairs. She was sat in one with the handcuffs threaded through iron loops in the sides, ensuring that sitting was about all she could do.

Sabien left her two hours ago, making some lame excuse about getting her files. She knew it was an interrogation tactic, one that was supposed to wear her down psychologically. It was kind of pointless, as she'd been ready to tell him everything the minute he showed up, but he never gave her the chance.

Caitlin had met the Protectorate once before: on the day that her parents had disappeared. They'd seemed so terrifying to a ten-year-old girl, appearing out of thin air in their stillsuits, their heads covered in the dark-lensed masks and weapons drawn. She'd hidden under the stairs, and it had taken Rufius over an hour to find her.

She could tell from half-heard conversations that there had been some kind of accident, but no one would explain what had happened to her parents. Total strangers came and went from her house. Some were relatives she'd never met, like great aunts with pinched faces, while others were more official-looking. And then grandfather turned up with his entourage, ordering his doctor to give Caitlin something to calm her until she fell asleep.

The drug had disrupted the memories of that time, making it impossible to go back into that part of her life. Lyra claimed that the cognitive maps were still there, but there was too much interference — she called it 'transience'.

The Protectorate took away a lot of their things over the next few days. She could still remember watching as boxes of books and documents were packed up and taken away.

Her grandfather had tried to get her to leave the house, but she refused. 'In case they came back,' she would protest tearfully.

Rufius convinced him that he would stay and look after her. Her grandfather was the head of the Scriptorian guild; he couldn't abandon his post to look after his only granddaughter even if he wanted to.

And he didn't.

It took Rufius three months to get her to leave the house. She didn't come out of her bedroom for the first four weeks, but he never gave up. Every day he would try some new tactic and every day she would throw it back in his face. There were times when she could hear him crying in the hall outside her door and she would bury her head in the pillow and do the same.

But she never cried in front of him, not then anyway.

Then one day he brought her a puppy. She called him Scout, and everything changed.

Scout didn't care about her parents or her pain. He just loved her unconditionally, every day, licking away the tears and eating her sandwiches when she forgot to put them high enough out of his reach.

The dog was her best friend, and slowly she came back to life.

'How long have you been visiting Master Zillers?' Sabien began.

'Two years,' she answered curtly.

'Before you joined the Scriptorians?'

'Yes. He was a friend of my grandfather.'

'Grandmaster Berinon Makepiece. I remember him well.'

'He'd probably never heard of you.'

Sabien smiled. 'And on the night of the murder, you were the one who picked up the staff?'

Caitlin remembered the way Zillers had relied on his staff. He called it 'old reliable'.

'I was scared. I thought I could use it as a weapon — before I saw the monster.'

'Yes, let's talk about this so-called monster. You described it to the xenobiologists as —' He consulted his notes. 'Like it used to be a man.'

'You were there the whole time? Spying on us?'

He nodded. 'That's part of my job.'

'I can think of another word for it.'

'But you didn't see it actually kill the curator?'

She shook her head. 'I didn't need to. It was pretty

obvious from the way it was carving that symbol into his chest that it killed him.'

Sabien stopped writing and looked up from his notes.

'What kind of symbol?'

'I only saw it for a second. I can't be sure.'

He flicked back through his notebook and turned it towards her. There was a carefully drawn sketch of the symbol.

'Do you know what this is?'

Caitlin felt the tears well in her eyes. She nodded. 'Akkadian.'

His eyes widened. 'Do you know what it means?'

She leaned in closer and focused on the sketch.

'Forger — I think.'

Quickly, he turned to a different page and showed her another symbol. 'And this one?'

Caitlin shook her head. 'No idea.'

He turned to a third symbol and again she shrugged.

Sabien closed the book, his expression turning grave.

'But I do know someone who would,' she said quietly. 'My tutor. Master Dorrowkind.'

28

SHADOWS

[New York. Date: 11.876]

When Kaori and Lyra appeared in the darkened salon of Madame Delawney, the cat was at the mirror, moaning and pawing at its blackened surface.

'It's the reflection,' Kaori suggested. 'He won't leave it — thinks it's another cat.'

'No, it's not that,' said Lyra, inspecting the glass. 'This is an obsidian mirror.'

'A what?'

'You haven't read Belsarus' work on mirrors?'

Kaori shrugged. 'Guess not.'

'He had a theory about the frequencies of reality. That we oscillate at a certain rate and that affects how we experience time — many people thought he was crazy, but if you read his work properly it is quite inspired.'

'And what has it got to do with mirrors?' Kaori asked, pulling Schrödinger back by his collar.

'I can't remember the exact process, but his general theory was that an obsidian mirror could be tuned to allow you to enter another dimension. He called them the "Shadow realms" — I think he had a touch of the dramatic.'

'Well, whatever you call it, Schrödinger hates it.'

Lyra bent down and ruffled the cat's neck. 'Cats have a keen sense for the paranormal. He's probably seeing something we can't perceive. I can try to read him if you like.'

Kaori frowned. 'No, it's okay. I'll take your word for it.'

Lyra shrugged and stood up. 'I think the Madrigor probably used it to enter the continuum.'

'You seriously believe that this shadow realm exists?'

'Oh, yes. Belsarus disappeared after his last experiment. There are those that believe he finally found a way to move into the future, and others, like myself, who think he shifted into another realm.' She placed her hand on the glass and began to play with the timelines it produced.

Kaori snatched her hand away. 'Or he just blew himself out of existence. I think it's better if we leave this to the experts — like Doctor Dangerfield.'

'If you say so,' Lyra agreed, holding onto Kaori's hand for a little too long. 'Oh my, now that is interesting.'

'Don't!' she said angrily, taking her hand away. 'What is it with you seers? You can't just go reading someone without their permission.'

Lyra's eyes widened. 'What is it? Is it from the maelstrom?'

'It's none of your goddam business.'

29

LANGUAGE

Master Dorrowkind looked guilty from the moment they entered his office. Caitlin had never seen him look so nervous, not even in front of Rufius. There was something about Sabien's arrogance that put people on edge. He seemed to see through them, and it was very disturbing.

'What has she done now?' Dorrowkind demanded, trying to deflect the conversation away from himself.

'That is still to be determined,' replied Sabien dryly.

Dorrowkind's office was looking remarkably tidy compared to the last two visits. Caitlin took some pleasure from the fact that he'd continued to use her indexing system on his other shelves — a small moment of victory in an otherwise dismal day.

'We're here to discuss languages,' Sabien continued, taking out his notebook. 'More specifically, dead ones.'

Dorrowkind looked visibly relieved; his brow unfurrowed and his pudgy fingers ceased their fiddling with his ladder chains.

'Languages, one of my specialities. Which ones in particular?'

Sabien held up the first Arkaddian character, and Caitlin realised that it was a test, to see if she was telling the truth.

Dorrowkind took out several pairs of spectacles and proceeded to put them all on.

'Looks remarkably similar to Sumerian cuneiform,' he said, squinting at the page. 'No wait, if I'm not mistaken that's Arkaddian.'

Caitlin smiled inwardly.

'And what does it say?' Sabien asked impatiently.

'Forger — as in one who makes forgeries rather than forges metal.'

Sabien nodded, showing no sign of emotion and turned to the next page. 'And this?'

Dorrowkind looked puzzled. 'That's a tricky one,' he said, pulling himself out of his chair and walking over to one of his bookshelves. 'Could be early Babylonian.'

He took down a large leather volume and flicked through the pages. 'Yes, it's the symbol for "tools", or more precisely, "tool-maker".'

Sabien wrote a note next to the symbol in a fluid copperplate and then presented the third.

Dorrowkind put the book down with a thump. His jaw went slack and his skin paled, as if he'd seen a ghost.

'Master?' Sabien asked, a slight note of concern in his voice.

The man sat down heavily in his chair, and took off his glasses.

'Where did you find that sigil?' he asked.

'I'm not a liberty to say.'

'I've only seen that pictographic style once before in all my years as a Scriptorian. I pray I never have to see it again.'

'What is it?' Sabien put the notebook down in front of the old man.

Dorrowkind picked up the book, his hands shaking as he pointed towards the symbol.

'That is a shadow rune, from one of the forbidden books in the restricted section: Belsarus' *Codex Arcanuum*. I believe it's a part of a harmonic, but you would need to speak to Doctor Dangerfield — he's the expert on that book.'

30

FOUNDER

[Richmond, England. Date: 11.558]

Rufius had never been a great one for waiting nor having to deal with authority — two personality traits that had somewhat hampered his career in ways that he couldn't be bothered to worry about.

Except when it involved the only thing he ever cared for.

Caitlin was the closest thing he'd had to family. She'd shaped the last seven years of his life — bringing him back from the edge of despair. Two lost souls with nothing left to live for. They had healed each other.

He dedicated his life to her safety, teaching her how to survive in the harsh reality of the continuum, and giving her the skills to help her deal with the crap that it was going to throw at her. Instead of barbie dolls and teddy bears he gave her colt .45s and Kung Fu. Rufius didn't know any other way. He had no idea if her parents would have approved, but they were as good as dead — so he just did what he thought was best.

Until the Protectorate took her away.

They were something he couldn't control. He'd spent so long teaching her about the external dangers, he hadn't prepared her for the internal ones.

As he paced outside the offices of the founder, Rufius tried to think of the best way to approach his old friend, Lord Dee, the man who had discovered him in the slums of a Viking York and saved him. In those days he'd assumed that Dee was just some kind of Shaman; little did he know the world he was about to enter.

'The founder will see you now,' the secretary informed him in a superior tone.

'Rufius!' Dee greeted him warmly. 'How are you my friend?'

'Not well.'

His office was located in the palace of Elizabeth I at Richmond. Lord Dee was her Astrologer General, not a difficult position for the founder of their Order, one who had an intimate knowledge of the events of the next five-hundred years.

Dee waved to a chair and poured out two large glasses of port. 'Come, sit and tell me what ails you.'

Rufius took the drink but remained standing. 'I don't have time for pleasant chit-chat, my Lord. They've taken Caitlin.'

Dee looked concerned. 'Who has?'

'The bloody Protectorate. Some inspector called Sabien.'

'And why would the Protectorate be wanting to talk to Caitlin?'

'That's exactly what I was trying to ascertain when he arrested her,' Rufius said, knocking back his drink and banging his glass down on the desk.

The founder took his seat and steepled his fingers against his chin.

'Have you spoken to Ravana?'

'Why on earth would I want to speak to that harridan?'

'Because she's the head of his department?'

Rufius sneered. 'I don't recognise her authority.'

The founder laughed. 'This has to end, you know. This feud between you has caused me no end of problems.'

'As soon as she admits she was wrong,' Rufius said, crossing his arms. 'Right now all I care about is getting Caitlin back.'

'And you think I can facilitate that?'

'Well, you're the head of the bloody Order, so you have the authority.'

Dee looked at him directly. 'In all our years have you ever known me to go against the rule of law?'

Rufius considered the question for a while.

'No. But —'

'But nothing. If the Protectorate have her, it will be for good reason — no matter how unjust you think it may be. They're following rules that you helped to create. Just because you decided to shirk all responsibility and wander the timelines as a man of the Watch, doesn't give you the right to come back and claim special privileges when it suits you. You gave that up a long, long time ago my friend.'

Rufius glared at him. 'I'm warning you something evil is on the loose and the Protectorate are going around arresting innocent people instead of protecting them. If you're going to stand by and allow it to happen, that's your choice, but I can't. I have to try and save her — no matter what it takes.'

Rufius hated the Protectorate with every fibre of his being. They were everything he abhorred about authority: inflexible, rules-obsessed jobsworths who had traded in their humanity for a system of rules and codes — if there was one who epitomised their narrow-minded bureaucracy, it was Ravana Eckhart.

They had run into each other on a number of occasions, the most recent being after Caitlin's parents had gone missing, when she had kept Rufius and Caitlin apart for six hours while they 'processed' the data from the house.

But that was not the worst by far.

She was the woman who had stopped him from saving his wife and child, the one who had condemned them both to die in one of the worst cholera epidemics of the nineteenth century.

There were rules about disease, strict ones that he himself had created with the founder many years ago. She had argued that there was no way to be sure that a virus couldn't be carried back through time once inside the host. She convinced the Council that quarantine wasn't enough; in her opinion nothing should be allowed out of a contaminated time zone, and while they fought over it, his wife and baby contracted the virus and died, horribly.

It had taken another six months to persuade the Council to repeal her amendment, but by that time he had nothing left to bury. Everyone had been burned, and he wasn't allowed to go back and save her.

Ravana sat, stony-faced behind the marble-topped desk in her grand office. She eyed Rufius warily as he entered the room, as if preparing for him to pull a gun on her at any moment.

'Westinghouse,' she growled, 'what the hell are you doing here?'

Rufius walked up to her desk and dropped a document in front of her.

'You have Caitlin in custody. I want her released.'

The Chief Inquisitor looked over the papers, her nostrils flaring as she read.

'She's been questioned by homicide as an uncooperative witness. Are you suggesting we disrupt standard police procedure?'

Rufius placed his massive fists knuckles-down on the marble top, leaning forward, his teeth bared. 'You have no legal right to hold her, the law — my law — states that a member has the right to council or be released within two hours.'

When Ravana smiled it was like watching a snake preparing to strike.

'I'm afraid your law was amended three years ago, under the 'Preservation of Temporal Evidence Act', and we can hold her indefinitely. You should read your Hansard memorandums.'

'She's innocent!'

'That is for my officers to decide.'

'You're going to let her go or —'

'Or what?' she said, standing up. 'Are you about to threaten me, old man?'

Rufius glared at the woman. He only had one card up his sleeve, one that he had been saving for all those years.

'Or I tell the founder what I know about your husband's hunting accident.'

Her eyes narrowed; she was weighing up the options. It was nothing more than a tiny signal, a chink in her armour, but it was all he needed.

'I'm not sure if the punishment for patricide has changed, but last time I looked it was a minimum sentence of life — a total redaction of the timeline.'

Her expression softened. 'It was an unfortunate accident, and the boar would have killed them both if my son hadn't shot first. Dalton would never have harmed his own father.'

It was his turn to smile.

'Except I have a witness who will testify otherwise.'

Her lips went white as she tried to hide her anger. They were old enemies and traded so many bitter words that she could tell he wasn't bluffing.

'Fine,' she said, picking up a quill and signing the order. 'But you will give me the name of the witness.'

'Perhaps, one day,' Rufius said, picking up the release form. 'Or maybe I'll just forget I ever knew it.'

31

DANGERFIELD

Kaori loved Dangerfield's office. It was full of everything she could ever want to study. His shelves were full of bestiaries, mostly his own, and composed the collective knowledge of every storm-kin that had ever been discovered.

She waited patiently for him, letting her eyes wander around the collection. The skeleton of 'Monty' hung from the ceiling; it was the only specimen of Mantellisaurus in existence, and had taken him six years to piece the complex fragments of bone together. Kaori knew better than to touch anything in the room. The latent histories of most of the objects would take her to places that were strictly off-limits, even to her, but there was something about the freakish-dinosaur that intrigued her.

'Good morning,' he said, stepping out from a door in the wall of books, which immediately vanished. 'Still trying to chase my dinosaur I see?'

Kaori snatched her hand back instinctively and tried not to blush. 'He's magnificent.'

'And far too ancient to weave with,' said Dangerfield with

a knowing smile. He was carrying an old leather book, which he placed carefully on his desk before coming over to join Kaori.

'There is so much we don't know about our own past,' she mused, still staring at the fossilised bones. 'Don't you ever wonder what it would be like to go further back?'

He nodded. 'Many times. The Cryogenian has always held a special place in my affections. Six-hundred and thirty-five million years is a long way to go, so it would probably be a one-way ticket.'

'Yes, but it would be worth it.'

'Perhaps when I retire,' he said, sighing and sitting down in his chair. 'So, to what do I owe the pleasure of your company today?'

'I have an interesting case — a murder.'

His eyebrows lifted. 'Really? How intriguing. Who?'

'His name was Zillers.'

Dangerfield eyes widened slightly as if he recognised the name. 'And he was?'

'A Scriptorian working back in Alexandria. It has all the hallmarks of a ritual attack.'

He steepled his fingers against his beard, which was long and almost completely white now. When Kaori had first met him it had been nothing more than a black goatee.

He shook his head. 'And why do you think that?'

'There was a witness, and what she described was definitely storm-kin. I had the techs do a full sweep, but found little in the way of traceable material. There was something odd though…'

'Hence your unexpected visit,' he replied, opening his hands.

Kaori paused for a moment, unsure as to how to phrase her next question. 'There was a connection to Belsarus. Schrödinger traced the creature back to the home of a linear who'd been experimenting with an obsidian mirror.'

Dangerfield tensed at the words, which wasn't the reaction that she was expecting.

'And the nature of the murder?'

She wasn't sure how much to tell him, as his reaction had put her on her guard. 'The Protectorate has only just released the pathologists report. They point to compression trauma of the skull. I think it was a mind rape, classic Monad absorption technique, but there was no obvious sign of a breach. Apparently the lensmen drew a blank.'

Dangerfield's tone hardened. 'Have you run the usual deviation tests?'

'Of course — they're all within tolerance. This isn't showing any signs of a maelstrom intercession.'

His hand went to the leather book, as though someone were about to steal it.

'Check again,' he ordered.

'But — '

'This has nothing to do with Belsarus, Dr Shika. You know the procedure. I expect you to follow the chain of evidence, and not waste time on his experimental theories.'

32

LE TRAIN BLEU

Rufius was waiting at the reception desk when they escorted her out of the Protectorate offices.

He had that concerned look he got whenever she'd been in trouble, as if he couldn't decide to be angry or caring and compassionate. They had an unspoken understanding that they would never discuss blame or fault, and whatever had happened was in the past and not to be dwelled upon.

'Are you alright?'

She nodded.

'Where do you want to go for lunch?'

'Somewhere far from here.'

'Paris?'

[Gare de Lyon, France. Date: 11.901]

Le Train Bleu was the most exquisite jewel box of a restaurant. Decorated for the Exposition Universalle in 11.900 by twenty-seven different artists, the luxurious gilded carvings and chandeliers always made Caitlin feel like a princess, and if you chose the right year there was a good chance of meeting Coco Chanel or Bridget Bardot.

They used to come here before taking the train down to the south of France. Rufius always said it was good to travel like a linear every now and then, just to remind themselves of what it was like for normal people.

She always ordered onion soup, and he had lamb. Food was an important part of their rituals, perhaps because Rufius liked it so much. It was the only time she ever saw him sit still, and always the best time to have a proper conversation.

'What did he ask you?' asked the old man, tucking his napkin into his waistcoat.

'Mostly stuff about how I knew Zillers, and about the symbols.'

'The one on his chest?'

She nodded as the waiter brought her soup.

Large cheese-topped croutons floated in the dark brown broth. It was without doubt one of her most favourite comfort foods.

'I think there have been other murders,' she whispered.

'Really?' he said with a mouthful of lamb.

'Sabien had other symbols. He showed me three, but I only knew the first one, "the forger". So we went to see Master Dorrowkind.'

Rufius laughed. 'I bet the old fart nearly died when you showed up with a Protectorate in tow.'

She smiled. 'He wasn't that pleased to see us, but when he saw the last symbol he went deathly pale.'

'Why was that?'

'I don't know for sure, it was something to do with Belsarus and a Codex — he called it a shadow rune.'

'Never heard of it.' Rufius shrugged and carved off another chunk of meat.

'No, neither had I. There was another symbol, "toolmaker", but Sabien wouldn't tell us where that was from.'

'Never trust 'em.' He poured out a large glass of red wine. 'They're too secretive for my liking. Not what we created them for.'

'You created the Protectorate?'

'A long time ago. Before Ravana got her talons into it. Eat your soup, it's getting cold.'

Caitlin swirled the brown liquid, letting the croutons swim around her spoon as she wondered about what other parts of his past she didn't know.

33

THE ROYAL SOCIETY

[Royal Society, London. Date: 11.752]

Sabien sat on the back benches, trapped between two portly gentleman who were discussing the upcoming presentation as though he wasn't there.

'The man's a complete fool,' said the first in a hoarse whisper.

'Have you read the abstract?' the other asked, waving a pamphlet in front of Sabien's face. 'He has the audacity to cite the founder on three occasions!'

The first man, whose long grey beard was tucked into his waistcoat, shook his head. 'Tore mine up on the way in.'

The auditorium of the Royal Society was a small, semi-circular lecture theatre with ranked seats that ascended steeply into the ceiling. The Order's Scientific Advancement Committee met every month in the mid-eighteenth century to consider new theories and presentations. They were an eclectic mix of philosophers and thinkers gathered from all parts of the Order, each with their own unique perspective on the science of time.

The Victorian theatre was lit by incandescent lamps that burned with a sulphurous orange glow. A small wooden dais sat at floor level, on which stood a series of metal spheres reminiscent of the Van de Graaf generators that Sabien had seen used in demonstrations of electrical current.

'Thinks he's a bloody Faraday,' the clean-shaven man grumbled, nodding at the spheres. 'Prepare yourself for a shock or two.'

'If he doesn't blow himself into the maelstrom, and us along with him,' said the other with a chuckle.

Sabien tried to ignore their bickering. He was here to see Belsarus, or at least to see what happened to the man on this fateful night.

The pamphlet was printed with the title 'Paradox' in large block capitals, and underneath the image of the two-headed Greek god, Chronos, the words 'Travelling beyond the Frontier', in italics.

The room was full of academics in evening dress, virtually all men, although he did spot the odd lady, one of whom looked remarkably like Maddox. But it wasn't her — she was already dead.

Belsarus walked out onto the wooden stage and bowed. The crowd's response was a mixture of cat-calls and heckling, the usual schoolboy welcome that everyone received at these events — no one liked a show-off.

He was a thin, gaunt man, with the haunted eyes of someone who slept little and took far too many opiates to stay awake.

The inventor cleared his throat. 'Gentleman, it is an honour to stand before you this evening and present my latest experiment.' He paused for effect, or applause, but got neither, and continued awkwardly under the glare of a hundred unimpressed faces.

'We have considered the subject of travelling into the

future to be the stuff of fanciful conjecture and impossibility.'

'Quite right!' heckled one of the crowd.

'Fairy tales!' cried another, getting a rumble of agreement.

'This, in my opinion, is retrograde thinking. My hypothesis is based on the fluidity of time, that unlike our current model of the continuum, there are indeed ways to traverse the frontier.' He raised his voice as the barracking became louder. 'That with the correct gravitational frequencies one may indeed be able to travel into the future without any repercussions!' He waved to an assistant, and a magic lantern show shone onto the white wall behind him as a picture of a flat earth came into focus.

'It wasn't so long ago that many believed the earth was flat, and that to travel too far south would end in one falling off the edge. As men of science, we must free ourselves of these limitations and seek to look beyond the boundaries.'

'Hear, hear!' came a lone voice, quickly stifled by his colleagues.

Encouraged by the outburst, Belsarus went on.

'I have to admit my previous experiments in gravitational frequency modulation have been fraught with disappointment.'

'Disaster more like!' interrupted someone, causing a peal of laughter.

'Regardless of these setbacks,' Belsarus continued, stuttering slightly, 'I have overcome many of the issues that beset my earlier prototypes and now have a fully functional machine.'

There was a general intake of breath.

'And no money left to run it!'

Another round of laughter rippled through the room, but Sabien sensed the mood was changing. The audience, including the two grumpy old men beside him, were leaning forwards and beginning to take notice.

'Theories of the Paradox abound, and none seem to agree on any part but one singular truth: that he or she will be able to travel into the future. I'm standing before you today to prove that with this device, you shall be the first to witness the paradoxical nature of time.'

He nodded to his assistant and the spheres began to rotate, first around their own axis, and then about each other.

Belsarus stood in the centre of the rig and let the charged metal balls sweep around him.

Small static discharges began to arc out from the devices, and the first two rows shrank back as their hair began to stand on end.

'There is no need for alarm, you're perfectly safe,' he shouted over the thrumming of the rapidly spinning spheres.

Everyone, including Sabien, could feel the influence of the magnetic fields oscillating out from the spheres. It was an impressive display of mechanical engineering, if nothing else.

Belsarus seemed to levitate, floating amongst the churning fields of energy. The crowd were enthralled as he closed his eyes and extended his arms. Everyone gaped as his body seemed to lose cohesion, beginning to phase in and out with reality.

Then something broke: a sphere came loose from its bracket and went flying over the heads of the crowd. Someone screamed as another came loose and everyone ducked for cover.

Sabien watched as Belsarus became solid once more and fell to the floor in a heap.

Assistants rushed in from the wings and tried to slow the spinning machine down, only to be struck to the ground or thrown sideways.

It quickly became a farce. Belsarus crawled off the stage and into the wings, the sound of fear and laughter ringing in his ears.

Sabien stood with the others and moved towards the end of the row.

'Terrible show,' muttered the bearded man.

'Paradox, my arse!' chuckled the other.

As he waited for the row to clear, Sabien caught sight of Doctor Dangerfield hurrying across the stage and into the wings. *So he knew Belsarus personally*, he noted.

34

AMBITIONS

Dangerfield could feel the moments of his life ebbing away. It was ironic that his stewardship of the Xenobiology department would end at the hands of the very thing it had been created to study — a creature of the maelstrom.

He had spent more than one lifetime trying to understand their origins and behaviour. Dangerfield had personally documented over four-hundred separate species, and developed a scientific foundation that had found hundreds more. They had worked tirelessly to classify the fauna of the chaotic realms and only just scratched the surface, limited by the difficult transition between their two worlds.

Ever since he could remember, he had wanted to explore the maelstrom, to step outside the continuum and never grow old, spending an eternity surrounded by the most fascinating void.

But it was an impossible dream — no one had ever returned from the chaos. Many Dreadnoughts had disappeared while fighting the breaches and none had ever made it back to tell their tale. Tachyons couldn't save them, nor did any of the other devices they had invented to safeguard them.

When Dangerfield first looked into the eyeless face of the creature, he'd known he would never realise his ambition. The two of them were standing in the middle of the non-corporeal section, the wings of frozen moths fluttering down like flakes of snow around them.

'What are you?' he wondered aloud.

Its mouth opened a little, as if to speak, but no words came. Just rows of crystal teeth and smoke-like breath that froze in the air between them.

At first, Dangerfield had assumed that one of their beasts had escaped, but in all his years studying them he had never seen such a creature.

The spines along its arms and across its skull were bony growths, disguising what was essentially a humanoid skeleton. Its eyes were missing and the nasal cavity was exposed, but it was still essentially hominid. The scientist in him couldn't help but be fascinated by the similarity; it was the first example of a corporeal biped.

He should have been afraid, and part of his brain was telling him that this thing meant to kill him, but there had been too many times when he had faced that danger, and he had grown so accustomed to it that it no longer affected him.

It paced around him, like a predator sizing up its prey. There was a strange aura about the creature as it prepared to strike. The freezing air caught an incorporeal element, a shape, like a shadow that trailed behind it. The faintest echo of a man, someone he recognised for the briefest second as the thing leapt forward.

Laying in the snow, he felt the creature's claws on his temples, something burrowing deep into his mind, looking for a memory and it was then that he realised who it was.

35

XENO DEPARTMENT

Sabien stood defiantly at the entrance to the Xenobiology hall, surrounded by a squad of Dreadnoughts.

'You have no business here,' one of the guards repeated, his gunsabre trained on Sabien's head.

'This is a Protectorate matter,' Sabien growled, his hand hovering over his sword. 'You have no authority to deny me access.'

'How about you try?' said a huge guard while stepping in front of his friend. The brute was nearly twice the size of Sabien.

The inspector instinctively tensed, sizing up his opponent for potential weaknesses.

'That won't be necessary,' came a woman's voice from behind the wall of muscle and armour. It was Doctor Shika.

Sabien relaxed slightly and smiled at the huge guard. 'Doctor, would you be so kind as to tell these gentleman to stand down?'

The wall of men parted and her sabre-tooth cat padded through, closely followed by the diminutive form of Kaori Shika — she looked as if she'd been crying.

'Inspector Sabien, to what do we owe the pleasure of your company today?'

'I need to speak with Doctor Dangerfield.'

She flinched at the sound of his name. Sabien had interviewed enough people to know when someone was hiding something.

'I'm afraid he's unavailable,' she said, but her reddened eyes spoke of something else.

'He's been hurt?' Sabien guessed, watching the muscles around her mouth twitch.

She looked down for a split second. 'Xenobiology is a dangerous vocation.'

He's dead, thought Sabien.

'When exactly were you going to report this?' Sabien asked, kneeling down beside the sheeted body.

Kaori and a group of xenobiologysts stood around looking cold and confused.

'We were waiting for Alixia. She's effectively in charge now that he's gone.'

'And you knew that once it got out your entire operation would be shut down.'

Kaori nodded. 'You already believe the creature escaped from one of our containment cells — isn't that why you're here?'

'So did it?'

'No,' she said, and sighed. 'All our live specimens are accounted for.'

Sabien looked around the frozen exhibits of twisted and ghoulish creatures. 'And the dead ones?'

'This wasn't one of ours,' she snapped. 'The marks are not consistent with anything we've ever seen.'

'Shame. I was hoping he would know,' Sabien muttered,

moving the sheet aside. Dangerfield's body was covered in ice crystals, and glittered as if he were covered in thousands of tiny diamonds. He pulled the sheet back further so he could examine the wounds. 'Do any of you know what that says?' He pointed at the symbol carved into the dead man's chest.

They shook their heads. Kaori had looked away, unable to stand the sight of her dead mentor.

The image was different to the others — more like a Chinese character. Sabien was beginning to regret letting Caitlin go, as she'd proved useful when it came to translations, but the orders from Chief Inquisitor Eckhart were pretty clear, and he had no reason to hold her. It was pretty obvious that the only thing she was guilty of was being in the wrong place at the wrong time.

Sabien replaced the sheet and got to his feet. 'I was actually here to ask him about Belsarus. I heard he was something of an expert?'

'He was an expert in many things,' Kaori said. 'Belsarus was more of a hobby.'

'I need to see his office.'

'Don't you need some kind of warrant?'

Sabien pulled out a slip of paper and handed it to her. 'Can we go now?'

The office was borrowed from a beautiful old reading room in the Bodleian. There were three floors of books, which could be reached via an elegantly carved wooden staircase that wound itself around the walls. In the centre of the room was a fossil skeleton of a large dinosaur.

In one wall was a large picture window. Its leaded panes

were filled with old glass; some were coloured and others had heraldic symbols etched into them.

In front of the window was a large desk, with various papers and letters scattered across it.

'What exactly are you looking for Inspector?' asked Kaori, watching him intensely. Her cat looked ready to take him down.

Sabien had never liked animals, especially cats — they had an aloofness, that meant you were never quite sure if they were just here for the food.

'Anything on Belsarus?'

'Why the sudden interest in the old inventor?'

'It's part of an on-going investigation.'

'I tend to find things a lot faster when I know what I'm looking for,' she said sarcastically.

'The *Codex Arcanuum*, or anything relating to his frequency experiments.'

Kaori walked around the desk and sat down. 'Inspector, you and I both know those are forbidden documents. No one is legally allowed to possess such a thing.'

'And if everyone did what they were supposed to do, I would be out of a job.'

Kaori's eyes narrowed. 'We've nothing to hide,' she said, and opened her arms wide. 'You're welcome to search the entire collection.'

'Would I learn anything?'

She shrugged. 'Who knows? Patience and maybe a little humility.'

Sabien's eyes narrowed. 'I'm assuming you have a better idea?'

Kaori nodded. 'Yes, as a matter of fact I do. Shall we sit? I'll order some tea.'

36

FREQUENCIES

'There were two worlds', Belsarus had written in the frontispiece of his Codex. 'The one that most call 'reality' and others that follow it like a shadow'.

After his failed attempt at the Royal Society, he'd persevered and discovered a doorway into another dimension, and it was just as intriguing.

Unlike the maelstrom, which was nothing more than a realm of chaos outside of time, his shadow world was perfectly stable, although strangely broken in many other ways. It seemed to exist in parallel to the continuum, with the same basic physical laws bar one: time moved at a different speed to their own.

The magnetoscope experiment had left him on the other side of the mirror, looking out at the 'real' world. Belsarus found himself in a decaying timeline, and the entropy of this alternate dimension seemed to be higher than their own; his house was literally falling down around his ears.

Chimæra

He spent days wandering through the estate and surrounding countryside without seeing another soul. It was a perfectly solitary place and Belsarus was fascinated by the seemingly permanent state of night that overshadowed it. A cloudless star-filled sky spread over his head as he surveyed the land around his house.

There was food, although he never really felt that hungry. The meals were left as if their residents had simply got up from the table moments before, but it spoiled quickly and it became something of a game to find one that was suitably fresh enough to still be palatable.

Every 'day' he would return to the mirror, perplexed by how fast his own face was ageing. He calculated that at the current rate it would be less the two months before he would be dead.

The magnetoscope was beyond repair; the accelerated rate of decay had already corroded some of its vital components. Belsarus peered out at the other version of the 'real' and found himself wondering what it would take to get back there. He touched the surface of the glass and found that his hand could pass directly through it, like a sheet of water. He could see the liver spots disappearing from the papery skin on the back of his hand.

Tentatively, he put his arms through, feeling the vitality returning to them. Closing his eyes he forced himself through the surface, feeling the speed of time slow as he stepped back into his well-lit ballroom.

Less than an hour had passed since he'd left.

He rushed to his study, so many theories spinning around inside his head; the idea that parallel timelines could exist would make for a fascinating paper. The fact that he could prove that they ran at different speeds would win him the Institute's prize for science, and silence all those who'd called him a crackpot.

37

GATEWAY

Kaori was a skilful negotiator, and by the time they had reached a settlement on her involvement Sabien felt like he'd gone five rounds with a beautiful but deadly samurai.

She showed him the secret passage in the bookshelf that led directly to Dangerfield's research. The works of Belsarus were kept in his private museum. A collection of his books, remnants of old experimental devices and other memorabilia, were carefully stored away in glass cases. Hundreds of Dangerfield's journals were stacked on the shelves lining the walls, each one carefully indexed with a fanatical sense of order.

In the middle of the room was an exhibit that outshone all the others. Enclosed within a brass cage sat a heavy, black-edged grimoire. Like a book of days, it lay open, displaying a spread of yellowing pages covered in demonic formulae.

'The *Codex Arcanuum*,' Kaori whispered. 'One of the last.'

Two hours later, after trawling through his journals, she

announced, 'Gateway,' and tapped on the symbol in the middle of a complex hexagram.

Kaori showed Sabien the mark in one of Dangerfield's journals. Symbols and their translations were crammed onto the page in his obsessively neat handwriting — it looked like the work of an obsessive madman.

'This is just a load of occult bullshit!' Sabien said dismissively, pointing at the Arcanuum. His boss already had half the department searching for an escaped Xeno exhibit. 'The last thing we need right now is a bunch of hysterical occultists turning this into a freak show.'

Kaori put the journal down. 'Dangerfield didn't think so. He always believed that Belsarus had found something, although no one ever proved it.'

Sabien picked up one of the other notebooks and flicked through it. 'The man was clearly obsessed,' he said, pointing at a sketch of a dark mirror full of stars.

'If Dangerfield wasn't dead, he'd be a prime suspect right now. I believe someone killed a linear because of that book,' he said, and pointed at the Arcanuum. 'Who else would have access to it?'

'No one here,' Alixia said with a shrug. 'But there's another copy in the restricted section of the Library.'

Zillers, thought Sabien. Finally he might have a connection.

38

FORGER

After lunch with Rufius, Caitlin couldn't go home. The word 'forger' kept bouncing around in her head. She'd known Zillers for two years and there was nothing false about him. He was a kind old man who'd shared stories about his life, his work and the wife he'd lost to cancer.

She was angry and confused. He had been her friend and didn't deserve to die that way. Carving an Arkaddian symbol into his chest wasn't the action of a primitive creature doing it out of fear or hunger — it was leaving a message.

But what on earth had Zillers forged?

There was only one real way to know for sure: Sim was right, she would have to go into his timeline, and for that she needed something of his, something personal.

Caitlin considered asking Sim to help, but what she was about to do was forbidden — just like all those times she'd gone back to watch that last night with her parents. Retrograding into another's past was seen as an invasion of privacy — only the Protectorate was allowed to do that, and she guessed they already had.

It had never really occurred to Caitlin to ask what Zillers did outside of curating his maps. They'd talked about his past often enough, but never about what he did after work.

She stood in his one-room flat in 12.007 staring at all the small items of his life, the ones that the Protectorate had left behind. There wasn't much: knick-knacks and souvenirs that held so much meaning to him, and yet very little to anyone else. There was no good place to start; one keepsake looked just like another — until she touched them and opened up their past.

History unwound from the first memento, ribbons of energy weaving around her fingers imparting glimpses of moments from his past. A random slideshow of times and places flashed through her mind as she teased them out. There was nothing unusual in the first three that she tested — each one involved painful experiences that brought her close to tears.

Then she picked up his spectacles.

Discarded and innocuous, they sat on a stack of old notebooks as if Zillers had just put them down. They were bent and cracked, and had been repaired more than once. It was strange that she couldn't remember him ever wearing them.

The history of his glasses covered every day from the last ten years of his working life. There were thousands of nodes to weave through, and just as she was beginning to wonder if she shouldn't use something else, a cluster and a date made her pause — it was the day her parents had disappeared.

The records department was housed in a vast underground network. Ten times larger than the London Underground, it used steam trains to move Scriptorians through centuries of documents — beautiful old engines that were operated by the Antiquarian railways division.

Caitlin stood at the back of the carriage, hiding among the other commuters as she watched Zillers make his way to work.

'Byzantine,' the conductor's voice intoned over the speaker as the train slowed into a station decorated with ornate mosaics. Half the carriage got off, leaving Caitlin feeling exposed, but no one took any notice of her.

The locomotive pulled away, rocking everyone back and forth as it gathered speed. She was finding it hard not to stare at Zillers. He was engrossed in his almanac, the glasses perched on the end of his nose.

This was her third attempt at following him. The previous two tails had ended when he'd entered a restricted section of the Egyptian second dynasty. The first time there had been a large contingent of Dreadnoughts, the Draconian special defence service, guarding the entrance — checking everyone in and out. Her flimsy cover story about working on a research project for her grandfather didn't make it through the first checkpoint.

The second time she dropped back a few days and tried again, avoiding getting too close to the date when her parents had actually disappeared. There was an even larger military presence on that day and they were all on high alert.

Something had gone badly wrong. The Dreadnoughts were taking records away in large wooden boxes. Caitlin pretended to be registering for a temporary pass at the front desk as they were carried out under armed guard.

'Name?' asked the young scribe, looking up from his ledger.

'Makepiece, Caitlin Makepiece.'

She wondered whether it would have been wiser to use a false name.

She nodded towards the guards. 'What's going on?'

'Some kind of foul-up. They've been here for two days now,' he admitted, trying to impress her.

'Any idea why?'

The young man shrugged. 'You know the Dreadnoughts, law unto themselves. Only masters are allowed in.'

The third time, she chose a week after the event. The Dreadnoughts were gone and everything seemed to have gone back to normal. It was strange to see how quickly everyone had moved on from what must have been the most disruption they'd seen in their entire careers. Scriptorians were like extreme OCD sufferers — they hated change.

'Hello again,' said the desk scribe.

Caitlin smiled as she watched Zillers go through the entrance and up the stairs. 'Hi. I take it the Dreadnoughts found what they were looking for?'

The scribe put his finger to his lips. 'I've no idea what you're talking about.'

She nodded. 'Sorry, I must be mistaken.' She pulled out a list of books. 'My master requires some manuscripts from the second dynasty — he's working on the restoration of the Turin Royal Canon.'

The scribe's eyes widened. 'I've heard it's the most extensive list of Egyptian kings ever compiled.'

Caitlin nodded. It wasn't difficult to impress a Scriptorian if you knew what to say.

He took the list from her, nodding as he scanned down the lines. 'These will take a while to locate.'

'It's okay, I don't mind getting them myself.'

She'd written the list from memory, trying to mix accessible documents with ones that would have been classified or restricted — she just needed to get close to Zillers' office.

He read the list again, as if considering her request seriously.

'If it was up to me —' he started.

'My master will be disappointed if he finds out you made me wait.'

The scribe folded the paper, stamped it, and handed it back to her. 'Just stay out of Nynetjer,' he said, while his eyes told her something else completely.

The restricted section of the Egyptian archive was an impressive collection of kings treasures and papyrus scrolls, each one displayed in museum-like glass cabinets; sacred artefacts rescued from forgotten tombs by the extraction division, a team of archaeologists who could trace a needle back through the proverbial haystack.

Caitlin had taken the hint about Nynetjer, moving quietly through the other sections of the second dynasty until she reached the year 7.260. The Order used a Holocene calendar, one that started from the end of the last ice age — around ten thousand years BC. The second Egyptian dynasty may have been three millennia before Christ to the linears, but to the Order it was seven-thousand years into their chronology.

Caitlin was still having trouble coming to terms with the fact that Zillers was the archivist for the very period that her parents were exploring when they disappeared.

He would've worked closely with them; it was standard procedure for Nautonniers, the Draconian navigation division, to consult with the relevant Scriptorian expert for the era. They would have been here a few weeks before, looking at the same artefacts she was hiding behind right now.

And he never told me, she thought. Zillers had spent all that time with her and never said a thing. Suddenly, she realised that she didn't really know him at all.

There were a few scribes wandering round gathering documents for their masters. Caitlin kept her head down, pretending to check a drawer full of gilded scarab beetles.

By the time Zillers came out of his office, it was nearly lunchtime and she remembered how he'd spoken about a legendary canteen in the central archive.

'It served the best Sardinian formaggio marcio,' he told her once, though she couldn't quite understand why anyone would go crazy for a cheese made with live maggots.

She knew he would be gone for over an hour. Central was a ten-minute ride away and only if the line was clear — which it hardly ever was. The problem with steam locomotives was that the engine needed regular repairs, and shifting them back to the yards in the late Victorian took specialists who were notoriously hard to find.

Caitlin made her way to his office and stepped inside. Nobody locked their doors inside the archives; it was an academic institution, after all — knowledge was only restricted because of the paths it opened into the darker parts of history — which students notoriously used for fraternity initiations which always ended badly.

Zillers' office was meticulous. On his desk was a blotter, a primitive typewriter constructed from local materials, and a sketch of him and his wife standing in front of the pyramids. Behind the desk was an entire wall of small wooden drawers, each one labelled with a letter. Instinctively she went to the Ms, pulling the long wooden drawer out and flicking through the index cards until she came to her parents.

Their names were written in red ink, the standard for a deceased record. At this time they'd been missing for less than a week and Zillers had already given up on them. The card was nothing more than a list of reference numbers and codes. It was a linking card, and she recognised the system immediately.

She flexed the card; it was stiff, like it was brand new. Whatever he was accused of forging, she knew it had something to do with what he did here.

Caitlin went back to his desk and touched the keys on the typewriter. If she was going to find out what happened, she needed to see what their card was like before the incident.

39
EVIDENCE

The book at Madame Delawney's house was spoiled; the blood made it impossible to see what she was studying when she died. Sabien had gone back and searched the place from top to bottom, and the only thing that still felt wrong was the mirror.

Sabien hadn't really paid much attention to it the first time, as it was just another piece of arcane memorabilia in a house of a woman obsessed with the occult.

Now, as he studied it properly, he was fascinated by the way the darkened glass seemed to absorb light — giving virtually no reflection. The frame was classical, its gilding peeling away with age, and the silvering under the glass was blackened — making it virtually useless as a mirror. There was a crack running diagonally from the top right to bottom left, and small pieces of glass lay on the floor as if something had punctured it from behind.

Sabien picked up a shard and examined the edges. They were sharp, long serrations, the kind created by a hard impact from a weapon, like a bullet. He tried to identify where the piece had belonged in the missing part of the mirror. The damage was unusual in the fact that it was localised around one spot. When he checked the back of the frame he couldn't find an entry point — as though the shot had come from inside the glass.

Holding a torch in line with the hole he tried to estimate where the bullet would have gone, narrowing the beam to a spot on the opposite wall where a bookcase stood.

Sabien kept the light trained on the same spot as he made his way to the books.

There were hundreds of leather bound volumes, first editions and rare-looking manuals on every possible arcane philosophy. Madame Delawney was clearly fixated on the after-life. From what Sabien had gleaned in Hartz's report on her, she'd lost her rich husband after only five years and had never re-married — spending her time and a considerable fortune trying to contact her dead husband. He could never quite understand what it must be like to grieve like a linear; to have nothing but memories of a lost love seemed so limited. He could go back to Maddox any time he wanted — the fact he didn't made it even more painful.

He couldn't find any trace of a bullet.

A message appeared in his almanac from Kaori telling him to meet her at the garage, but he decided to ignore it for a while, trying not to look as if he was running to her whenever she clicked her fingers.

'What exactly are you looking for?' Sabien said sharply, watching the cat scent mark the wheel of an Oldsmobile.

'Schrödinger's looking for a scent, something the Draconians failed to do with their tech.'

'I'd rather concentrate on finding out why he was killed — that tends to work better for me,' he said sarcastically.

Kaori folded her arms. 'You have a problem with Xenos, don't you?'

He shrugged. 'Never seen a monad that didn't look better dead. Your department has never done anything to convince me otherwise.'

'So your answer to anything you don't understand is to kill it?'

'It's a low risk option. My job *is* to protect the members of the Order, after all.'

There was a fire in Kaori's eyes and her cheeks were flushed. 'You have no idea what we've learned, how many lives we've saved with our research.'

'Enlighten me,' he teased, looking at his watch. 'I'm not busy for the next ten minutes.'

She was about to react when her cat growled loudly at something beneath one of the cars.

They walked over and Kaori bent down and pulled out a metal object. It looked like a hip flask. Examining it more closely, she took out a small pair of forceps and pulled the tip of a claw out of the metal casing.

'This is exactly what I'm talking about: with this kind of material our lab could have a species type within a couple of hours.'

Sabien fished the jar from the autopsy out of his pocket and held it up.

'Would a whole one be better?'

'How long have you —'

'It's evidence. We do have forensic procedures of our own,' he said with a smile.

'And they came up with jack-all didn't they?' She snatched the glass bottle out of his hand. The claw shimmered in the light as if it was made of opal.

'It was translucent when we found it, but seems to be losing its opacity.'

'Where was it?'

'Embedded in the victim's chest.'

She chewed her lip as she slid the claw out of the tube and held it up to the light. 'Ripping tool. See the serrated inner edge, like a shark's tooth or the talon from a bird of prey.'

'Not a demon?'

'What?'

'Never mind.'

'Out of interest, what did Sergeant do?' she asked, nodding to his abandoned car.

'Antiquarian engineer. He built the tachyon MKIV — has a wife and family up in the thirties. I'm going to see her tomorrow. I'm assuming you don't want to tag along?'

Kaori shook her head, putting the claw away carefully. 'I need to get this back to the lab, before it degrades any further.'

40
GW25-299.1

'But what does it mean?' Lyra asked, leaning forward and taking the index card from Caitlin.

'It means that something was removed. Redacted from their record.'

'GW25-299.1,' she read out aloud. 'And it's definitely not on the later version.'

Caitlin shook her head, 'No. I checked, twice. That's an identifier for some kind of record, but I don't recognise the system. It's either something Zillers dreamt up himself or —' She froze mid-sentence.

'Or what?'

'Or is from an older collection, pre-Mayerstein.'

'You're losing me.'

Caitlin took the card back and looked at the file references. 'Do you see how these all start with a prefix of three letters then a dash? That's Mayerstein's classification category: "SCI" is science, "BIO" for Biology, and so on.'

'Okay. And GW25 is an older way of doing it. So don't we just go back to the system before?'

Caitlin sighed. 'Trouble is, there wasn't just one. Before

Mayerstein there were five different systems; it wasn't a great time in the Scriptorium. Fights used to break out in the stacks between rival indexers.'

Lyra laughed. 'Sorry, but I can't imagine what a fight between two librarians would look like. Did they hit each other with bookmarks?'

Caitlin ignored her friend and studied the numbers, racking her brain to think what it could be.

'Don't you think it would be easier to ask the Draconians?'

'Why?'

'Well, you said they took away hundreds of documents. Maybe the thing you're looking for is in there. Your godfather is a senior member of the guild after all.'

'But the creature marked Zillers as the forger, and no Draconians have been killed, have they?'

'Not that we know of.'

'I need to find someone who knows about the old indexes.'

'Master Dorrowkind?'

Caitlin grimaced. 'Not if I can avoid it. I think between Rufius and Sabien he may feel less inclined towards helping me.'

Lyra smirked. 'I'm not sure who I'd be more scared of.'

'Yeah,' Caitlin said, and smiled. 'I think Dorrowkind nearly wet himself when I showed up with the Protectorate.'

41

NEXT OF KIN

[Colchester, Vermont. Date: 11.932]

Sabien wasn't often surprised by a relative's reaction. He'd lost count of the number of times he'd been the bearer of bad news; there were only so many ways that the grief presented itself: tears, anger, disbelief — he had seen them all. It was a terrible thing to have to tell another person that their beloved had died, and even worse to witness their reaction.

Usually the sight of a Protectorate officer on your doorstep in the middle of the night was enough, but still there were those who were so in denial that he had to explain it in detail — sometimes more than once.

The Sergeants owned a white clapperboard house on Lake Champion, near the centre of Colchester. America in the early thirties was an unusual choice for a couple to pick, but Sergeant's wife was a Copernican studying the economics of the great depression. The living arrangements felt a little weird to Sabien; having your husband working ten years away during the week seemed to point towards problems with the marriage.

When she opened the front door he could tell she already knew. There was a stoicism in the way she set her jaw and a slight redness around her eyes that all spoke of grief.

'You've had a wasted journey,' she said, holding the door to let him in. 'I know he's gone.'

It was a refreshing change to not have to say the words. Though in some kind of ritualistic way they were still waiting to be said, stuck in the back of his throat.

'My sympathies,' was all he could manage.

She nodded and showed him into the lounge.

'Do you want something to drink?' she asked, picking up a tumbler half-full of clear amber liquid.

She's a drinker, noted Sabien. It was only ten-thirty in the morning.

He shook his head and took out his almanac. 'I just have a few questions, trying to get a better picture of who he was.'

Davies and his team had been through the official records: Sergeant was a genius, completing his apprenticeship by sixteen, and was the youngest master of Antiquarian engineering and his career was a glowing record of invention and achievement right through his thirties and into his forties. Then something happened. Davies called it his 'mid-life crisis'. There was a gap in his record that no one could account for, when he came back to work and took a lower position on a project that he should have been directing.

'What do you want to know?' asked his wife, lighting a cigarette. She was wearing a yellow dress, and her hair and make-up looked to Sabien like she was preparing to go out on a date.

Possible affair? he scribbled in his almanac.

'Did he have any problems at work?'

She laughed. 'We never spoke about his work. Weekends were sacred — it's what kept us together so long.'

Sabien pretended to make some notes. 'Can you think of anyone or anything that happened over the years that he may have got in trouble over?'

Her eyes glazed over a little. 'You mean since he quit his job?'

'He quit his job?' Sabien said, trying to sound surprised. This was why he had come; he needed to fill in the gaps.

'That's why we moved back here — I thought it would be on his record.'

Sabien shrugged. 'You know how slow Copernicans can be. They're still collating the data. When exactly did he resign?'

She put down the glass and stubbed out the cigarette. 'Twelve years ago he just walked in and announced he'd quit. Never said why. Later he got a draughtsman position on the tachyon upgrade and we moved back to the twenties. The hours were long and I never settled there. So ten years ago we bought this place. It's got a great view of the lake, don't you think?' She walked over to the window, trying to hide the tears that were streaming down her face. 'We have a boat, called *Serendipity*, and he used to love spending the weekends out on the water.'

Her shoulders shook as she tried to control the sobs.

'Do you know what he was working on before the tachyon V?'

'No, only about his boss, Jaeger, but never about what it was. It changed him.'

Sabien made his excuses and left.

42

GRANDFATHER

[China. Date: 9.790]

The sculpture of the Chinese water dragon hovered majestically over the still surface of the pool, its serpentine body silvered by the moonlight. Caitlin could still remember the day her grandfather had released the two carp into the pond, as a memorial to her parents.

She always found it easier to think here. It was a peaceful place, somewhere she would come to reflect and meditate.

She'd spent most of the day going through all of the different indexing systems and couldn't find anything that matched. The code was annoying — like an itch she couldn't scratch.

Caitlin was out of ideas.

All she knew was that Zillers had hidden something about her parents and the Draconians were involved somehow.

Her godfather, Emilio Derado, was a senior member of the Draconian High Command. Every year, since her thirteenth birthday, Derado had invited her to join the guild, and each time she'd turned him down.

Everything about the Draconians reminded her of the day she'd lost her parents; she blamed them for the disappearance, and nothing could ever persuade her to ask them for help — not even this.

But she had tried everything; there was nothing else she could think of to do.

She looked down at her reflection and wondered how many tears she'd wept into the water. The fish swam lazily to the surface; over the years they'd become used to her, taking food from her hands.

Caitlin let her fingers linger in the water, felt their cold mouths eagerly searching for a morsel. They used to give her some comfort, when she was younger, but now they were nothing more than hungry fish. She reached up and touched the sculpture, the cold stone chilling her to the bone — like touching death.

It was a vestige, connecting two simple points in time. At the other end of its timeline was another dragon, waiting in the atrium of the Lighthouse, the Draconian headquarters. Its twin was a Firedrake: a magnificent fire dragon and the path to a godfather whom she hadn't spoken to in nearly five years.

Derado was an ambitious man who had dedicated his life to the cause. He had no other family and had been one of her parents' closest friends. When they disappeared something seemed to change in him. He avoided Caitlin, making excuses about important meetings and missing birthdays, but he always sent a card — and within it the invitation to join them.

She pulled her hand back from the timeline before it

drew her in. It felt too much like she was giving up. If Derado did know something about her parents then he had kept it from her all these years, and that made him complicit — if he didn't, then he was no use to her at all.

She looked down at the fish, swimming leisurely around their tiny sanctuary, unaware of the world beyond the edges of their kingdom. Caitlin felt as though she was being kept inside a walled garden, that there were too many things she didn't know.

And she realised there was only one person who would always tell her the truth.

Grandfather.

Inside this room, Caitlin reminded herself, *are the minds of every grandmaster that ever lived.*

Glowing like old radio valves in the darkened chamber, their preserved brains floating in domed jars of formaldehyde and electrolytes, the grey matter of the Order's most powerful leaders sat in silence.

'Are you sure you want to do this?' asked Sim, surveying the morbid row of pickled brains.

'He will know,' she replied, touching the label on her grandfather's jar. She picked it up carefully and carried it to the table in the centre of the room.

'It still freaks me out,' Sim said, unwinding the cables from the throne-like chair that sat beside the table.

Caitlin sat down and pulled her hair back and tied it in a pony tail. 'You're a Copernican, so anything that's not finite freaks you out.'

'But hooking up to a dead man's brain! Wouldn't you rather read his books?'

'It'll take too long.' She placed the net of copper electrodes over her head. 'Anyway, he's my grandfather, it's not like I'm going into the mind of a complete stranger.'

The process was known as 'Intuiting' and was common practice among the guilds for passing on knowledge — except for the Copernicans of course, who shunned it entirely, believing it to corrupt their faculties. *But then they don't even like holding hands*, she thought.

'Each to their own,' said Sim, attaching the cables to the metal contacts on the sides of the jar.

Bubbles formed on the inside of the glass as the connection between Caitlin and her grandfather opened.

WHO/WHAT/WHERE/WHEN

The usual tirade of mental questioning came, the words forming directly in her mind. It was like waking a child from a deep sleep.

The preserved had no concept of the passage of time, some of them having lain dormant for hundreds of years. Her grandfather had died when she was twelve, two years after her parents had disappeared.

He'd spent most of the time looking for his daughter, leaving Caitlin in the care of his best friends Rufius and Alixia. The unexplained disappearance of his only child had changed him, and he was forced to step down from his role as Scriptorian grandmaster: his mental and physical health suffered badly and two years of unfruitful searching took their toll.

She made the usual response.
GRANDFATHER -> JUILANA -> CAITLIN
DAUGHTER?
GRANDDAUGHTER!

She opened her memory to him, sharing the moments from her childhood. The times they had spent together in the grand palaces and ancient museums of antiquity. Times before he had become so important, before he forgot about her. There was a slight pause as his neural network recognised the information.

CAITLIN. WHERE IS MOTHER?

She knew this would come. It was a question that had died on his lips in the hospital bed. Caitlin couldn't ever forget the way he used to look expectantly past her whenever she entered the room, a frail old man waiting for the rest of the family.

GONE GRANDFATHER

His mind was still waking, but she could sense his memories of her mother beneath his consciousness, embedded under the surface like precious jewels in a riverbed. She caught glimpses of her as a young woman, a similar age to Caitlin, and then older with a baby in her arms — they were out of sequence and random, but still beautiful moments.

MISSING GRANDDAUGHTER

It was hard to tell whether he meant he missed Caitlin or her mother was just missing. There was no emotional context to his words.

She had to remind herself that this was no longer a man, but a series of preserved electrons stored in a biological medium — like a computer, she just had to ask it the right question.

REQUEST INFORMATION
BEGIN.
WHAT IS GW25-299.1?

There was another delay. Caitlin noticed she was holding her breath, and let it out with a sigh.

'You okay?' Sim touched her hand.

Caitlin nodded and closed her eyes.

RECORDS GW25-299.1 CLASSIFIED - TOP SECRET

The response came. It was obviously buried deep within his memory. She didn't have the clearance to access it; even in death they managed to maintain a level of secrecy. She tried another tack.

WHERE IS RECORD GW25-299.1?

This time the memory surfaced, and she entered it. There was a long corridor in a storeroom buried deep underground. She walked along it in her grandfather's mind, reading the labels on the many boxes and books, finding nothing usable, nothing that would give her the location. She knew there were hundreds of hidden archives.

A temporal location appeared.

-10.001 25.0° 12.12°

'Shit!' said Caitlin, and her eyes snapped open.

'What?' Sim looked concerned.

'They've hidden it at the end of the last ice age!'

43

LABORATORY

Kaori took the claw out of the vial, clamped it onto the rotatable mount, and switched on the examination lamps.

The laboratory was empty. The death of Doctor Dangerfield had hit many of the staff hard and Alixia De Freis, who had stepped in as acting head, had given them all some compassionate leave. Kaori's assistant, Bellamy, had taken Schrödinger off to the Mesolithic to chase pre-historic Zebra, giving her the perfect opportunity to work on her reconstruction in peace.

The lab was fitted with some highly specialised technology, one of the benefits of being annexed to the Draconians. Their artificers didn't have the same level of temporal expertise as the Antiquarians, but still had some pretty kick-ass gadgets when it came to cellular re-sequencing.

Unlike the rest of the order, the Xenobiology department was situated as close to the frontier as possible, which meant they could use the latest technologies: computers, AI and a hundred other diagnostic tools — as well as hot showers and Xbox.

She booted up the control system and the 3D laser scanners went to work on the claw. Fine lines of red light flickered over its surface while it rotated slowly on the base.

Pouring herself a cup of hot coffee, Kaori watched the image build up section by section on the large OLED screens.

Spectrometric data began to appear next to the model of the claw, the graphical chemical analysis showing her exactly what it was made of.

'Not shark,' she said, sipping her drink. She put the cup down and pulled a stool over to her workstation. 'Okay. Let's start with the terrestrial.' She dragged the chemical profile onto another screen with a swipe of her finger and initiated a search of the known holotypes on their database. While she loved the old-fashioned bestiaries that Dangerfield had written and illustrated by hand, there was nothing quite as efficient as a CRAY IV for pattern matching a million different compounds.

NO MATCH.

The response flashed on the screen.

'As expected,' she murmured to herself. 'Now the xenoforms.'

The response took slightly longer this time, but with the same result.

She frowned. 'Neither fish nor foul.'

The DNA analysis flicked up onto a third screen, and was a more positive result. The thing had enough organic material to run a simulation. The estimate began to countdown from ten hours.

'Shit,' she said, and pushed back from the desk. Ten hours was a long time to wait when something that dangerous was on the loose. Not that Sabien was entirely convinced it was a beast at all — he was still looking for a motive, and she guessed it was just the way he was wired.

Chimæra

For some reason she felt obligated to prove it to him, not because he was some thick-necked copper, but because the honour of the department was at stake. Dangerfield had spent his life establishing this science, and she didn't want it to get forgotten in all the chaos of his murder.

There was a process to follow, an empirical approach to classifying and understanding this creature, and she wanted to be the one to complete it.

44

SIM

Sim stared at the date Caitlin had written down when she came out of the intuit. Her skin was pale, and her hair was plastered to her scalp where the net of electrodes had sat.

'What's back there?' he asked.

'The truth,' she said, and sighed, knowing that there was no way to reach it without a special warrant from the founder. No one was allowed back beyond zero — ten-thousand-years BC. The timelines before that date were too chaotic, too dangerous for everyone but the Nautonniers, the exploration division of the Draconians.

'No chance of getting to that then. You'd need a pretty serious vestige to hit that date. The probability is less than half-a-percent on anything pre-zero.'

He was right, of course, Caitlin knew. Vestiges from pre-history were hard to come by. Finding a man-made object that matched a specific date was very unlikely that far back; so much of the material from those times was based on natural resources like bone, stone and wood that it made it too dangerous to use. Natural materials had a tendency to take you to places you never intended to visit. They were too random to use accurately — there were a few that could, and were sarcastically referred to as 'Druids'.

Sim put the brain back with the others, tapping the glass with his finger as if it were a fish in a tank.

'So how was Grandpa?'

'Still looking for mum,' Caitlin said glumly, standing up and running her fingers through her hair. 'I need a bath.'

He pulled a face. 'Yeah, you do.'

She punched him hard on the arm. 'You're not helping.'

'Not sure who can.'

'Oh, I know someone who can get back there,' she replied with a cheeky glint in her eye.

Sim thought for a moment and then his eyes lit up. 'Of course.'

45

DIFFERENCE ENGINE

[Hall of Copernicus. Date: 11.580]

Why had Sergeant quit his job? Sabien pondered as he walked into the Copernican's central hall the next day. The wunderkind responsible for some of the most important innovations in tachyon development had failed so badly that he felt the need to walk away. Something didn't feel right, which generally meant it wasn't.

'Inspector,' said a tall, gaunt man in a long black robe.

'Professor Eddington.' Sabien bowed slightly.

'May I interest you in a short tour? It's not often we have the pleasure of a visit from the Protectorate.'

Sabien declined. There was a lack of emotion in Eddington's voice that made it impossible to tell whether he was being sincere.

'As you wish. Shall we?' The professor turned towards the nearest elevator and signalled to one of the operators to call one down.

'We don't often get requests of this type — my computational team have spent most of the last two days preparing the cards. They're quite excited to see it run.'

Eddington's voice was so dry and monotone. Sabien wasn't sure what constituted fun for a Copernican, but their Christmas parties must have been a blast.

They travelled high into the upper levels of the hall, passing up through the gearing of the enormous difference engine that permeated every floor. It was like moving through the workings of an enormous clock, Copernican engineers dodging between the many moving parts with oil cans and wrenches, keeping the machine in permanent motion.

The Clackers, as the Copernican statisticians were more commonly known, stood on brass platforms taking down numbers, or feeding punched cards into slots and adjusting dials — each of them checking and rechecking the figures on slide rules and elaborate abacuses.

Sabien looked up to the glass roof, still high above them, the stained glass colouring the sunlight that filtered through it. It was hard to believe they were under the Thames, and he tried not to imagine the force of the water bearing down on the glass. Nor what would happen should the pressure within the hall change and allow the river in.

A small bell chimed and the elevator came to a stop.

'Data retrieval,' intoned Eddington.

A young man pulled back the safety cage and bowed to them as they stepped out.

'Inspector Sabien, this is Simion De Freis, actuary first class, and he will be running the program for you today.'

They shook hands. 'You're Methuselah's boy?' asked Sabien, holding on to his hand a little too long.

'Yes,' replied Sim.

'I worked with him a long time ago.'

Sim's eyes widened slightly. 'Oh, I see,' he said nervously. There was an awkward silence.

'Shall we?' Eddington asked, motioning towards a large set of doors.

The data retrieval room had a domed ceiling which was lit by a spherical projector installed in the centre of the floor, like something from a planetarium.

'We've run the preliminaries,' Sim advised the professor, who simply nodded.

There were four or five other people in the room, who moved between consoles making their final adjustments and muttering under their breath about the sequencing.

'The subject in question is Henery Sergeant,' instructed Eddington in a loud and dominant voice, something that surprised Sabien entirely.

'We need a timeline trace protocol that reaches back… Sorry Inspector, how far do you wish us to run the search?'

'Twelve years.'

'Time span of three-point-seven to the eighth, with temporal deviations of plus or minus two percent and bayesian pruning on bifurcations of more than two to the twentieth.'

As he spoke, the team were busy adjusting their controls and Eddington swept around the room checking their configurations.

'Simeon, the cards, if you please.'

Sim took out a large stack of white cards from a velvet lined wooden box and placed them on a shelf at the base of the brass projector.

He pulled a lever and the cards descended into the

bowels of the machine, lights illuminating under the glass floor to reveal thousands of gears turning through a hundred different combinations per second, as they processed the cards.

The noises of the machinery drowned their voices, but Sabien could just make out the sound of Eddington giving course corrections to his team. It seemed to be a stream of numbers and formulae, the language of temporal mechanics.

A light flared inside the central projector and lines of data were beamed out onto the surface of the dome above them.

Sabien watched as temporal charts and probabilities flashed over its surface, too fast to be read, every data point ever recorded scrolled across the ceiling.

At the centre of the hemisphere was a date, the number descending rapidly as the search ran back through time in minutes, and he watched the digits slowly crawl back towards the date Sergeant had left. As it reached the relevant moment the data began to slow, shifting and scaling as the engine focussed in on its subject.

Then it stopped.

There in the cluster of all that was Sergeant's life, a finely traced network of lines connecting variables, factors, and a thousand other things that influenced his timeline, was a dense cluster of data.

'Expand nexus four-theta,' ordered Eddington.

The projection zoomed into the cluster and the details separated out, unpacking themselves to create a cloud of other events and people.

'What is that?' Sabien asked, squinting at the detail.

'Project Osirion,' murmured Eddington. 'There are many redactions, something we usually associate with a classified record.'

The names and associations were blurred or blacked out

so that all that they could make out were some requisition orders that Sergeant had made for extra equipment and a few supply chain dockets.

The light in the projector winked out.

'That's the end of the run,' Sim explained. 'Our compute window has expired.'

Sabien had more questions, but knew his time was up. Whatever Sergeant was doing it was top secret, which meant he would have to go higher up the chain of command — something that was going to get him noticed by all the wrong departments, and that was the last thing he needed right now.

46

IMPOSSIBLE

Caitlin found Rufius in the kitchen. The cook, Mrs Bottomley, was tutting and fussing around him as he prepared something that looked remotely like a stew.

'Hungarian goulash,' he said, holding a wooden spoon up for Caitlin to taste. 'Needs a little more paprika I think.'

Caitlin sampled the food and nodded. 'And caraway.'

The old man began rifling through the herb jars, much to the chagrin of the flustered cook.

'How could I forget the caraway seeds! Where are the little buggers? What kind of system is this?'

'Mine,' growled Mrs Bottomley, handing him a metal tin of seeds clearly marked with the label 'Caraway'.

Rufius measured a handful of them out into his palm and delicately sprinkled them into the large pot, stirring them in slowly.

For as long as Caitlin could remember her adopted uncle had loved cooking. He said that it relaxed him, and judging by the size of his belly, he didn't mind the eating of it either. Rufius was a big man, well over six-feet with a large bushy beard, and she'd never really been sure of his age. He'd always looked the same to her, but he must have been in his sixties, at least physically speaking. Members of the Order tended to live a lot longer than normal, linear people — the founder was rumoured to be nearly a thousand-years-old, but no one ever bothered to check, as longevity came with the job.

'Can I have a word?' Caitlin whispered to him while Mrs Bottomley was clearing up the seeds he'd spilled all over the table. 'In private.'

'Well?' Rufius asked impatiently, standing on the back steps looking out over the garden. 'Something tells me you've been up to your usual tricks.'

She grinned. 'I need to ask a favour, a really big one.'

'Are there such things as small ones where you're concerned?'

'How many times have you been back beyond zero?'

His eyes narrowed a little, suspicion gathering in the creases of his forehead. 'Too many — why?'

She took out her almanac and turned to the page, showing him the date. 'Have you ever been back that far?'

He whistled through his teeth. 'Negative ten k. You really aren't messing around are you? What's there?'

'Some kind of storage facility.'

'A secret facility, to be more precise.'

'They're hiding something about mum and dad. I think it has something to do with the day they disappeared.'

Rufius looked puzzled. 'Why would they hide something about the breach?'

She shrugged. 'I don't know, but they took a lot of stuff away the day after it happened, and when Zillers updated the record for my parents he left something out.'

'And you know this how?'

She tried to hide the guilt, but failed miserably.

'You've been back into his timeline?'

'Purely as an observer,' she said, holding up her hands.

He scratched at his beard. 'And then how exactly did you trace it back to this secret archive?'

This was the conversation she'd wanted to avoid. They'd had many debates over her grandfather donating his mind to the guild. It was something she and Rufius had disagreed on for years.

'I asked grandfather.' Inwardly, she shrank as she said it.

'You what? After everything you said —'

'I know,' she interrupted. 'But the index code was old, and no one else knew them like grandfather did.'

'You actually asked me to steal him once. Do you remember? You told me to throw him into the sea!'

'I was fourteen! No kid says stuff they mean at that age. Don't you remember what it was like?'

Rufius glared at her. 'No, I don't. However, I do remember what you were like.' He pulled up the sleeve on his jacket to reveal a pair of long white scars. 'I have the scars to prove it.'

'That was the dog's fault,' Caitlin protested. 'So, will you help me?'

He rolled down his sleeve. 'Do I have any choice?'

She put her arms around his neck and buried her head in his shoulder. 'Thank you.'

'One of these days child, you're going to ask the impossible.'

47

NIGHT RUN

The forest was haunting at night. Giant trunks loomed out of the darkness as his tachyon caught them in its light. He was running fast, his bare feet crushing the pine needles as he pounded through the ancient forest.

Breathing hard, Sabien pushed on through the pain in his legs. It was mile fourteen and the cramps were getting worse. There was still another hour of running to get back to the eighteenth century and he was a long way from the right tree.

He loved running in the dark; he found it helped him to focus his mind on the elements of a case. There was something bothering him about the murders and he couldn't put his finger on it.

Everyone in the department was laying bets on it being some nightmarish creature from the maelstrom. With the Xenos involved things had got more complicated and the whole investigation had ground to a halt — as he knew it would.

Sabien knew this was more than some sporadic killing

spree. There was a motive and it had something to do with Belsarus — he just couldn't work out what it was.

There were no records of Project Osirion, or at least nothing his security clearance would allow him access to. Whatever classified work Sergeant had been involved in, it was going to be hard to prove any connection to Zillers or Dangerfield, but three out of the four victims had something to do with Belsarus, or at least one of his books, and that was still his best option.

Without noticing, he'd run deep into the past, using the timelines of ancient Yews and Oaks to take him back thousands of years. By the size of the metasequoias around him now he estimated he'd gone back over thirty-thousand years this time — the furthest back he'd ever been and totally forbidden within the Order.

The calls of the night creatures filled the forest with strange sounds, as though he had wandered onto some alien planet — a dangerous one full of unseen predators.

He stepped up the pace, running his hand along the bark of random trunks as he passed, jumping hundreds of years at a time as he made his way back up the millennia.

It was nearly dawn by the time he reappeared from the woods. Panting and covered in sweat, he walked the last mile across the common, letting the early morning mist cool his skin.

A herd of deer were grazing in the grounds at the back of his house, and they eyed him suspiciously as he wandered casually across the scrub towards the gate.

Richmond Park was a beautiful part of the world to live

in, and in the eighteenth century it was still unspoilt and the view of London from the top of the hill was breathtaking.

The house was quiet when he entered. He pulled off his vest and took a towel from the back of a chair, wiping the sweat off his face.

'You took your time,' came a woman's voice.

Kaori Shika was sitting at the kitchen table.

'How?'

'Doesn't matter,' she said, admiring the tattoo that ran across his sweat-soaked chest. 'Get dressed. There's something I need to show you.'

48

ICE CAVES

[British Museum. Date: 11.923]

The British Museum after closing time was one of Caitlin's favourite places. She and Rufius had spent many hours walking the halls, discussing the exhibits and planning their next adventures.

Following him through the labyrinth of glass cases, Caitlin felt like a child once more. She remembered how he'd cared for her when all the others were running around shouting at each other, trying to find a reason for what had happened.

'Roofuss', as she used to call him through gappy teeth, was the one who had focused on her needs. He invented the games that kept a ten-year-old from dwelling on her missing parents, and one of his best was the treasure hunt.

He would hide something sweet amongst the exhibits — chocolate buttons to begin with — and sent her off with a set of cryptic clues. She would roam the empty halls trying to decipher the codes, and without knowing it, learning every nook and cranny of the museum, or at least how it was in 11.923.

It was the time of Carter and the Tutankhamen excavation and the contents of his tomb were a magnificent centrepiece of the museum. A lost civilisation's treasures were displayed in all their golden glory. Even now as they passed through it, she still had to pause to appreciate the magnificent sarcophagi of the boy-king.

The games had grown more complicated and devious as she got older. No longer contained within the museum itself, they began to range out into the past. Using artefacts from the exhibits, she would find herself in the most random parts of history, and it was no longer chocolate she was hunting for, but treasure. He called her his 'Jackdaw', for she loved the shiny things.

Looking back now, she knew it was all a training exercise; the clever and gradual education of a master watchman. He'd been teaching her everything he knew, and it had been just the distraction that she needed.

'Are we going to use room fifty-one?' she asked, knowing exactly where the oldest artefacts would be.

'No, thirty-two,' he said, reaching the stairs. 'We need Scott's diary.'

Caitlin was confused. She knew artefacts from the Quartarian ice age would be rare and most would be nothing more than tools and animal bones, but she couldn't quite work out how Scott's Antarctic expedition would take them further back than 11.912.

His tone reminded her that this wasn't a game. What she'd asked him to do could land both of them in front of the Star Chamber — the high court of the Order.

Draconians were the only ones allowed to travel outside of the continuum, which covered the last twelve thousand years, carefully modelled by the Copernicans using the maps of the Draconians' Nautonniers. The danger of going back so far was change. The further back you travelled the more significant even the smallest alteration could be to history — everything was magnified by time.

The twelve millennia were carefully monitored; it was a safe zone in an otherwise chaotic and dangerous past. The most difficult part of navigating back before the continuum was the lack of artefacts.

Nestling in the lofty roof garrets of the museum were stored the diaries of Scott's last expedition. Rufius opened the display case and took one carefully from its velvet lined drawer.

'The Draconians will have their own way of getting there, I dare say,' he muttered, holding the small notebook up into the light and squinting into it.

'Won't it be cold?' Caitlin asked. They were wearing the Order's standard travelling robes, made from a dark jute-like substance that wasn't designed for Antarctic conditions.

'We won't be out in the open for long,' he said, as his hand weaved over the journal, teasing out the timeline.

'But didn't he get trapped in a terrible blizzard and die of exposure?'

'You've dealt with worse.'

He was referring to the time she'd fallen through the ice when they were on one of his "adventures" on Svalbard, inside the Arctic Circle. The water had been so cold that she had gone into hypothermic shock almost immediately. Ironically, it has saved her life. The rescue team had taken far too long to fish her out, and she was clinically dead for over ten minutes.

Caitlin had never seen a grown man cry quite as much as Rufius had done that day.

[Cape Evans Hut. Date: 6th June 11.911]

Caitlin stamped her feet on the bare boards in a vain attempt to shake the cold that was creeping through the soles of her boots. The hut was like a freezer, as cold winds blew through the gaps in the windows and rattled the glass.

'What are we doing here exactly?' she asked, blowing into her cupped hands.

'It's Scott's forty-third birthday,' Rufius explained, looking out of the window.

There were a group of men kicking a ball around in the snow, watched over by a large team of huskies and very cold looking ponies — it was the strangest game of football Caitlin had ever seen.

'And we came to wish him a happy birthday?'

'No,' he scowled. 'We came to get this.' He picked up a kit bag with the name 'Frank Debenham' stencilled on the canvas.

'Debenham was a geologist, and if I'm not mistaken has collected more than enough samples for what we need.'

'You're going to use a natural?'

The colonel ignored her, tipping the contents out onto one of the unmade bunk beds. An eclectic collection of volcanic glass and other rock samples scattered across the sleeping bag.

'What exactly are you looking for?'

'Anything from the Koettlitz Glacier. A Gneiss, or a Schist, anything with quartz or feldspar should do, or preferably a metal if we're lucky.'

There was a shout from outside as one of the teams scored. She watched them all patting each other on the back and generally enjoying the weak sunshine. It was hard to imagine that some of them would never make it back or that Scott's attempt to find the South Pole would fail.

She could feel her body temperature dropping and was beginning to shiver uncontrollably when Rufius finally found a viable sample. It had been cut in half and she could see the striations created by a hundred thousand years of pressure. At the centre was a fine vein of gold.

'This should do fine,' he said, stroking off the dust with his thumb.

[McMurdo Sound, Antarctica. Date: -10.001]

The sun warmed Caitlin's face as she looked across McMurdo Sound. There was no sign of the Ross ice shelf. It was just as Zillers' old charts had described; a coastline free of ice lay before her, carved out of the granite by millions of years of glacial erosion.

'Warm enough for you?' Rufius asked, walking back up the beach. He looked dreadfully tired; the last jump seemed to have sapped all his energy.

Caitlin nodded. She wondered what Zillers would have made of this place, and then a thought suddenly struck her: was it just a coincidence that he was researching the exact same location as the hidden Draconian facility? *Probably not.*

All that time he'd been searching for the same thing, but the question she couldn't answer was why.

'Come on,' he said, his beard flecked with ice — it was still only just above freezing. 'We've got a hike ahead of us. We need to make the Mount Erebus by dark.'

She looked up towards the vast, snow-covered mountain range and wondered how far back Rufius could have travelled with the vein of gold.

The corridors she'd seen in her grandfather's memory were actually ice caves carved into the permanent ice pack, and they stretched for miles into the glacier.

Caitlin shivered uncontrollably as they marched down into the dark. The temperature inside the ice was quite mild, but she couldn't shake the chill that got into her bones from the ten-kilometre walk through the snow to get there.

'Why ice?' she wondered aloud.

'Untraceable,' Rufius replied, his voice echoing down the glassy tunnel.

She blew on her hands, pins and needles shooting through her fingertips as the blood began to flow.

'Keep them inside your coat, close to your body,' he advised. 'Don't want them warming up too fast.'

The entrance hadn't been guarded, nor was their any sign of habitation as they moved further inside. Rufius used the light of his tachyon to illuminate their path when the daylight petered out.

'Did he give you any idea as to where they might have hidden it?' Rufius asked, standing at an intersection where the mouths of three dark tunnels gaped before him.

Around each of the bore holes were carved a series of beautiful scenes. Someone had taken their work seriously, sculpting trees and woodland creatures into the ice walls. Above each entrance was a symbol, which Caitlin recognised from her mother's Draconian signals manual.

'Take the left,' she said, pointing to the one marked with a hieroglyph that looked a little like a bird with a spear through its chest.

'Why that one?'

She shrugged. 'Because it says top secret?'

Rufius looked confused, swinging his torch over the

symbols of the other two. 'So what does that say?' he asked, picking one of the others out with a torch.

'Latrines.'

He shrugged and marched off into the left hand portal.

Caitlin was relieved he didn't ask her about the central symbol. It looked remarkably like the glyph for 'Plague'.

After half a kilometre they came to the first set of storage areas. They were packed full of wooden boxes, each one stencilled with an official seal and a reference number.

'GWR1001.2' the old man said, reading off the first one he came to.

'Close.'

'Assuming they've been packed in order that is.'

She went to the next room and found that they were.

It took another hour to locate the box, sitting unremarkably amongst a hundred other similar crates, covered in ice and left to rot in the middle of a glacier. Caitlin hesitated as she felt the rough wood against her fingers.

'Do you want to do the honours?' asked Rufius, holding up an ancient looking flint axe.

'Where did you get that from?'

He grinned. 'Always come prepared for a fight —'

'— and leave with your balls intact,' she completed his old mantra. It was one of the things he used to say to her every time they went on an adventure — supposedly for luck. It was not something that most ten-year-old girls would be expected to repeat, but it made her smile every time.

She took the axe and used it to lever open the lid. Whoever had packed this had used something like lead to seal the box. It refused to budge for her and it took a combined effort between the two of them to crack it.

Caitlin wasn't sure what she was expecting to find inside. As far as she could work out, the straw-filled container seemed to be full of unusual mechanical parts. She checked the number on the side and it was definitely the correct box.

'What is it?'

Rufius picked out a couple of old brass gear wheels and a panel which looked more like a piece of armour.

'I think the correct question is — what was it?'

He was right. It was broken, whatever it had been before, and was now just a jumble of components.

'Your mother was a good mechanic, but this looks more like Antiquarian engineering,' he observed, laying them out on the floor like a jigsaw puzzle.

Caitlin picked one out and inspected it closely.

'There's a masters' mark on it,' she said, holding it up for him to see.

III-VI-MXII

'Three, six, one-thousand and twelve,' he translated with a shrug. 'Not much to go on.'

Caitlin stroked the inscription, feeling the time unwind from it. 'Well, there's one way to know for sure.'

Rufius snatched it out of her hand. 'No you don't, young lady. If anyone's going to go weaving into unknown timelines it should be me.'

He rubbed his thumb over the metal stamp and she watched the deep lines furrow between his eyes as they closed. Ribbons of time expanded out from it, looping around his fingers as he searched through its past. There was a twinge in his cheek, like he'd bitten into a sour fruit. His teeth bared slightly and he sucked in a sharp breath, then his eyes snapped open.

'Rufius?'

He wasn't there. His eyes were glazed, fixed on the scenes from another time. His hands were shaking, knuckles white where he gripped the metal.

'Rufius, stop it! You're scaring me!'

But he couldn't stop it. The veins on his temples were raised and sweat was forming on his brow.

'Don't t-t-touch!' he growled through clenched teeth.

Caitlin looked around for something to knock it out of his hand and saw the axe.

He sank to his knees, white spittle drooling from one side of his mouth. She brought the axe down on the metal, smashing it out of his hand and across the icy floor.

The connection broken, he fell backwards and his body went limp — lifeless on the cold ground.

She knelt beside him and felt for a pulse. Her hands were numb, still half-frozen from their journey, and it took a nervous few seconds for her to register the weak beat of his heart.

'Rufius?' she whispered. 'Can you hear me?'

There was no response.

49

CHIMÆRA

The holographic model of the creature rotated slowly on the table in front of Sabien. Standing at half a metre high it was an impressive looking beast; full-size, it would have scared the shit out of anyone.

The body was covered in some kind of scaly skin, like one of those dogs with no fur. There were bones protruding from its spine and skull as though it had been put together badly. The head was by far the worst part, and any sign of humanity had been eradicated. The thing was completely blind; the eye sockets were gone and there was just a remnant of a nose. It was like looking at someone that had survived a terrible fire.

'It's a Chimæra,' explained Kaori, walking around from the other side of the table.

'Does it take you long to come up with these names?'

She ignored his remark, tapping a series of buttons on the table's surface.

Sabien had never seen technology like this; the frontier wasn't somewhere he liked to spend too much time. It was fraught with danger, both linear and non-linear. The Copernicans predicted the twenty-first century was going to be the most violent period in history, and the electrical fields, Wi-Fi and radio signals were all an anathema to his natural abilities.

'It's a combination of two separate species, a hybrid, but one that couldn't occur naturally.'

'Like a liger?'

'Kind of.'

The hologram shifted and separated into two figures; one was a human, the other a terrible beast that looked like an armoured dog.

'What the hell is that?'

Kaori liked the way he spoke so directly; there was no subtlety about him. 'That's a Cryptid, a particularly nasty parasite that feeds off breach energy. We've got a couple upstairs if you would like to see one in the flesh.'

He shook his head. 'So you're telling me that the perp is some kind of combination of these two?'

'That's what the DNA is telling us. The predictive modelling was close, but I had to make a few artistic corrections based on what Caitlin described.'

She moved the two models aside with the wave of her hand and the Chimæra returned to the centre spot.

Sabien went around to look at the man. His face was generic, like a photo-fit, nothing he could use to identify him.

'Do you know who he was?'

Kaori shook her head. 'Nothing matches on the Order's database, but then not everyone has been tagged.'

'You think he's from the Protectorate?'

'Or someone who wants to remain untraceable — there aren't many other possibilities. I'm not sure how you would even create this kind of hybridisation. You'd have to be in close proximity to a breach to do it. Cryptids don't tend to wander too far from the maelstrom.'

'Have you ever heard of Project Osirion?'

She shook her head. Her jet-black hair was held up in a bun with a pen sticking out of it, and there were dark circles under her eyes from where she'd obviously worked all night.

'Have you eaten?' she asked.

He gave him an odd look, as if he wasn't expecting that particular question.

'No.'

'Neither have I. Let's go and find some breakfast.'

50

GODFATHER

Caitlin sat next to Rufius as he lay in the bed. She'd never been in this part of Bedlam; the hospital was spread over two-hundred years, and this period was obviously reserved for special cases or high risk prisoners — she couldn't quite decide which category they fell into.

He had been in a coma since they'd been rescued from the storage facility. The Draconians arrived moments after she had messaged her godfather. Such was the beauty of time travel, a note written twelve-thousand years before she was born instantly appeared in his almanac the second after she wrote it.

To say he was unhappy to find her in their most secret of storage facilities was an understatement. Only the critical state of Rufius saved her from a bollocking on the spot. The medics had taken them both into Bedlam immediately. Her hypothermia was bordering on severe, and whatever Rufius had experienced had knocked him for six.

After they had rewarmed her and treated her ice burns, Caitlin insisted on being taken to him. She felt guilty for whatever he'd suffered because of her, and couldn't imagine what could have done so much damage.

The nurses muttered as they went back and forth with various poultices and potions.

'Doctor Crooke wants them applied every twenty minutes, so see that you follow his instructions to the letter!' the sister barked at her staff.

Caitlin could tell it was serious, but no one was paying her any attention. She finally realised she wasn't welcome after an incident with a bedpan.

'Sorry miss,' apologised the young nurse, wiping down the floor with a cloth. 'Perhaps it would be better if you waited out yonder.'

From her speech, Caitlin guessed the woman was from the fifteenth century. She had the forearms of a milkmaid, strong and sure, and the plain complexion of someone who had never felt the brush of Rimmel or Max Factor.

The nurses of Bedlam were mostly recruited from local priories; the sisters were a reliable source of healers and asked little in the way of payment. None of them were of the Order. The Doctor, Helias Crooke, had insisted on using them when he'd taken over the role as director of the institution.

Caitlin took the hint and went out into the waiting room. Its walls were plain and uninspiring, and there was little in the way of distraction to stop her mind going back over the events at the ice cave. She tried to rationalise what had happened — what those device parts were for. Had her mother invented something? Why did the Draconians bury it in pre-history?

There were no answers, just more questions, and frustrated, she made her way out into the gardens.

Her godfather, Grandmaster Derado, was sitting in the sunlit quadrangle reading a book surrounded by the flowers and herbs of the hospital's small medicine garden.

It was strange to find him in such a peaceful place. Her memories of him had always been shrouded in formality and procedure, and as he had grown more powerful — a detail of fierce-looking guards.

Yet now he was alone.

'How is he?' he asked, taking off his spectacles and closing the book.

'No better,' she replied, sitting next to him on the bench. There was an overpowering smell of lavender and rosemary.

He breathed deeply. 'The damned fool will get himself killed one of these days.'

She tried not to cry. The last few hours had been a whirlwind of emotional trauma, and seeing Rufius so pale and vulnerable was something she was finding hard to deal with.

'Will he recover?'

'That my dear is in the hands of Doctor Crooke. Though there's no better physician, and since I've not yet met the thing that could best Rufius — I would hazard a yes.'

She felt a wave of relief wash over her.

'But that doesn't excuse your actions. What, may I ask, were you doing back there?'

Caitlin wasn't sure how much he already knew; his face was as inscrutable as ever — he was a consummate politician and a mean poker player, so she opted for the truth.

'I found a reference to something that Zillers left out of their record. Rufius was trying to help me with it.'

Derado, the most powerful member of the Draconian guild, turned towards her and spoke with fear in his voice. 'What I am about to tell you, god-daughter, is something that must remain between us, and us alone. Do you understand?'

She nodded.

He took a deep breath. 'There was a time when we knew little about the maelstrom and men, very brave men and women, volunteered to explore it, to venture outside the limits of the chronosphere so that we may learn more of the realms that lay beyond. These hardy souls were chosen for their ability to survive in the most extreme temporal conditions.'

'Like the Dreadnoughts?'

He smiled. 'Even more so. Anyway, these were dangerous, desperate times. There were frequent breaches and we lost members on a near daily basis.'

Caitlin couldn't imagine what it was like to live in such a world. Since her parents had disappeared, there had only been one or two breaches as far as she knew.

'There was a joint task force, known as Project Osirion, and the combined skills of all the guilds were brought together to create tools and techniques that the Order could use to fight the creatures of the maelstrom.'

'And my parents were part of this?'

'Yes, they were deployed to the twelfth century, for reasons best known to the project director, a man by the name of Jaeger. Your parents were involved in a vulnerability survey; the mapping of the weak points in the chronosphere.'

Caitlin remembered a map they'd pinned to the wall of their study. It was the most complicated chart she had ever seen, covered in multiple timelines, notes and pins. She'd marvelled at all the places and times they had been to — wishing that they would take her along on one of their missions.

Derado stood up and stretched his back. 'I want to show you something,' he said, adjusting his tachyon. 'I think you're old enough to see it now.'

He held out his hand; there was something different about him today. This was no longer the aloof old man that wouldn't come visit her on birthdays, but instead a witness to a part of her life that she'd hardly any memory of.

Childhood was supposed to be a golden time, Caitlin had read somewhere. One of the main reasons people looked back fondly on their 'formative' years was because the development of the brains gave them a selective memory. Not everything from those early years was retained. Events with high emotional content or stimulus had a better chance of making it into the deep centres of the brain, but it was something of a lottery.

Caitlin had been back into her own timeline many times, but there was still so much she didn't know about that era, things that a ten-year-old wasn't privy to. Her world at that age was a small bubble that encompassed the house, her school and a few trips into the past. She had no idea what her parents really did for a job, nor who those other strangers were that turned up in the middle of the night.

'Where are we going?' she asked, taking his hand.

'Somewhere I should have taken you a long time ago.'

'Egyptian architecture is an impressive thing to behold when viewed from the right century,' Rufius told her once when he took her to visit the excavation with Flinders Petrie and Howard Carter in 11.892.

At that time the relics of the Pharaohs were only just being unearthed. They were like children unwrapping Christmas presents, uncovering hidden treasure that had been lost for thousands of years.

Now, as Caitlin looked down over the glittering city of Abydos, she realised how truly magnificent and powerful the Egyptians had once been. Standing at the top of a dune, watching the Nile flow through the lush green valley, she found it difficult to reconcile it with the dry tombs that Petrie had discovered.

'So beautiful.'

Derado smiled. 'Isn't it? This is Abdju, but the Greeks called it Abydos. Home of the Royal Necropolis and the temple of Seti I.' He pointed at the grand buildings that stood at the centre of the city.

He took out the book he'd been reading in Bedlam; it was full of hieroglyphs. Caitlin recognised some of the text from the prayer for the dead.

'There's a reason this period is off-limits to most,' he said, holding the page up for her to see.

She translated the glyphs. 'Osiris?'

'God of the underworld. Abydos is the centre of a religion based on the worship of the dead, one that attracts a considerable amount of interest from the storm-kin.' He closed the book. 'In their pursuit of the afterlife, the Osirion priests have become rather skilful aperturists. Some of our experts think they may have latent temporal abilities — like those of our seers.'

'They've created a breach?'

He nodded. 'Small ones at first, all very containable, so we setup a permanent research station here, and used it to learn more about the maelstrom. It became our testing ground for new weapons and defence systems.'

'What did this have to do with my parents?'

He put the book away and took her hand. 'That's what I want to show you.'

The temple was deep below ground. Small oil lamps flickered in the corners of the long stone room, illuminating the faces of fierce-looking demons carved into the rock.

'This is the Osirion. One of the oldest temples of Osiris,' his voice echoed down the chamber. There were two Dreadnought officers standing guard at the entrance. They snapped to attention as he passed by.

'On February eleventh, during the feast of Osiris, we received reports of a significant breach. The monitoring station registered something close to a level seven — they'd never observed anything higher than a four.'

He walked down the centre aisle and Caitlin followed, already feeling the energy fields prickling at her skin. Ahead, where she assumed the altar used to be, a silver wall shimmered as if it were going in and out of phase.

'This was going to be our first test of a new defensive system. Everyone had been drilled and trained and we were confident that our equipment would prove more than capable of stopping whatever was attacking the continuum — how wrong we were.'

Rufius had told Caitlin that her parents were lost in a battle somewhere in the second dynasty, that it had been one of the worst ever recorded, but no one had told her when exactly and the whole period was quarantined.

'At approximately twenty-two hundred hours the first wave broke through. The battle lasted for over three days and we lost over a hundred souls.' He stood in front of the shimmering field. 'The bravery of officers like your mother and father saved the timeline, not to mention the future of the human race. Yet it's never been possible to close it, and the stasis field is nothing more than a sticking plaster while the boffins work on a more permanent solution.'

Caitlin stared through the field, trying to see what was on the other side; it was the closest she had ever been to the maelstrom. All she could see was a dark void, nothing but cold empty space beyond the shielding.

They weren't in there, she reminded herself. They were in

some other version of this timeline where none of it ever happened. Rufius had taught her to imagine that there was an alternate reality where they had never gone on the mission. Her fertile imagination had done the rest, creating a different history where they had come home and never left her again.

'So what was it that you were hiding back in the Palaeolithic?'

Derado sighed. 'There was an experimental programme — testing new equipment. The parts you found in storage were all that remains of an extraction system, a kind of a temporal parachute. It was supposed to bring them back from the maelstrom.' His expression soured. 'It failed miserably.'

'And Rufius has just witnessed the whole thing?'

Derado nodded. 'I'll be very surprised if my old friend ever wakes up again.'

51

BREAKFAST

[Piccadilly, London. Date: 11.874]

'I never saw you as a vegetarian,' said Kaori, tucking into her sushi.

'I'd have thought after all those dissections that you'd have been put off meat for life,' Sabien replied.

They were sitting in Kaori's favourite restaurant, the Criterion, in Piccadilly. It was an opulent, Neo-Byzantine dining room with gilded ceilings and arched, colonnaded walls.

'These maki are so good.' She grinned, devouring another seafood roll.

'I didn't know that the Victorians even knew what sushi was.'

She shook her head. 'This is one of the only places that do. The chef is from Kyoto. Came over in eighteen-sixty-four, and there are only a few customers he makes it for.'

Sabien looked at the artful design of the seaweed wrapped rolls and compared it to his bland looking grapefruit.

'Would you like to try one?' She held one up between her chopsticks. 'This one is just cucumber and radish.'

He nodded and opened his mouth so she could drop it in.

The taste was exquisite, until he bit down into the rice and tasted something hot.

'Eutrema japonicum!' she grinned as he winced. 'Should have warned you about the Wasabi. I'll get you some more.'

She called over the waiter, an Asian man dressed meticulously in a white jacket and gloves, and ordered another portion.

'Are you from this period?' Sabien asked as the man took away his food.

'No!' she said, and laughed. 'Far too backward for me. I was born after the Second World War. Dad was a GI and mum had a thing for men in uniform. He went back home, and I was brought up in post-war Japan. Not the best environment for a *hafu* to grow up in.'

'That explains the blue eyes,' Sabien joked.

'Yeah, kind of a giveaway,' she said, blushing. 'What about you? How long have you been in the Protectorate?'

'Since I was fifteen. I was born during the troubles in Northern Ireland. Dad was killed by the IRA in '72. I was recruited into the Order in '76 — never went back.' It was an easy lie, one he had told so many times it had become natural.

'Sounds like neither of us got a great start in life, but why join the police? That's not something most would opt for.'

Sabien shifted uncomfortably in his chair, looking sideways at the people on the surrounding tables.

Kaori feigned surprise. 'Sorry, are you undercover? Is this some kind of secret mission?' she whispered.

He shook his head. 'We don't like to draw attention to ourselves, and to answer your question — because I like solving puzzles.' His food arrived and Sabien picked up the chopsticks clumsily. 'Or maybe I've just read too many Sherlock Holmes stories.'

She took his hand and positioned the two sticks between his fingers.

'You know this restaurant featured in one of them?'

'A Study in Scarlet, although Conan-Doyle hasn't actually written it yet.'

'Now that freaks me out.'

'Why?' he asked, before taking a maki roll and stuffing it into his mouth, his eyes widening as the wasabi struck again.

'Temporal dissonance. I'm a scientist, I understand the logic behind the continuum, but the fact that I've read a story that hasn't even been written at this moment in time — it just messes with my head. I'd rather stick to my creatures any day.'

'Where is your cat, anyway?'

She looked around anxiously, as if she'd left him somewhere, and then smiled. 'He's with my husband. It's his day.'

'You never told me you were married.'

'I'm not, not anymore. Bellamy's taken him on a hunting trip back into the Mesolithic.'

'Bellamy —your assistant?'

'It's complicated.' She rolled her eyes. 'So what are you going to do about your Chimæra?' she asked, effortlessly changing the subject.

Sabien pushed his plate away. 'My creature? I think that honour belongs to you.'

'But now you know what it is can't you at least put out a warning or something? There's a danger to the public.'

Sabien took out his almanac. 'The warnings have already been posted. I don't believe these are random attacks. There's a reason why it's doing this and I think it's got something to do with Belsarus.'

She laughed. 'The mad inventor?'

'He was much more than that, and Dangerfield knew something about it. You know what this symbol means, don't you?' Sabien held up the sketch he'd made from the marks on Dangerfield's chest.

Kaori nodded. 'Kanshu. It means Jailer.'

Sabien made a note. 'And how many of your creatures have you known to leave a mark after they've killed.'

Kaori shrugged. 'None, as the storm-kin don't tend to leave much behind after they attack.'

'Exactly. Dangerfield was my best hope of finding out what all this mumbo-jumbo with the Codex Arcanuum was really about. With him gone all I have is a spooky old mirror, a dead librarian and a secret, classified project that's above my pay grade.'

'My money's on the mirror.'

'Not the secret project?'

'I was joking.'

52

III-VI-MXII

Caitlin looked pale and tired as she sat quietly across from them on a large leather sofa. Lyra had made one of her 'special' herbal brews, which tasted like a thousand different fruits had been blended into a hot chocolate.

'She went back how far?' Lyra asked in disbelief.

'Minus ten k,' Sim said proudly.

'And they let you go?'

'Kind of, but Derado made me wear this.' Caitlin held up her wrist, with a strange-looking silver bracelet wrapped around it.

'Tracer,' Sim observed. 'You're under observation.'

'Damn, girl,' said Lyra. 'You're in deep shit!'

Caitlin looked tearful.

'Not as deep as Rufius,' added Sim. 'He's still in a coma, and if he wakes up, I've heard they're going to throw the book at him.'

'Don't!' Caitlin's lip trembled.

'What happened to him?' asked Lyra.

Caitlin took a deep breath. 'He saw something bad —

something to do with my parents. I'm not supposed to talk about it.'

'And?' asked Sim eagerly.

Caitlin sighed. 'We found this equipment, from some kind of secret experiment they were involved with. Derado said it went wrong and they had to abandon the whole thing.'

Sim looked puzzled. 'What kind of equipment?'

'Metal, like a breastplate, but with dials like the Protectorate have on their stillsuits.' Caitlin thought back to the maker's mark on the equipment. 'And there was a mark, Roman numerals, stamped on it.'

'Maker's mark,' smiled Sim. 'Can you remember the sequence?'

The assay office of the Antiquarians was like an Aladdin's cave: gold and silver treasures lined the shelves, each one carefully labelled with the details of its origin.

'Can I help you?' asked a small man standing behind the wide glass-fronted desk. He had wiry grey hair, large white whiskers and wore a bright red waistcoat beneath his finely-tailored guild robes.

'Yes,' said Sim, clearing his throat. 'We wish to trace a maker's mark.'

The man smiled and waved them forward. 'If you would like to show me the item?' he asked, holding out one hand while picking up a pair of complex spectacles with the other.

'We don't actually have it,' said Caitlin, realising it sounded a little crazy.

'Oh?' The man sounded disappointed. 'That may make things a little more complicated.'

'I have the details,' Caitlin explained. 'It's a series of

Roman numerals,' she added, handing the assayer a slip of paper.

He squinted at the numbers before giving up and putting on his reading spectacles.

'Ah. Yes. Indeed,' he muttered, holding the note up to the light.

'Do you know who this might be?'

The old man laughed. 'Well, of course! I have some of his finest work right here,' he said, pointing to a tray of tachyons beneath the glass. 'This is none other than Henery Sergeant, Artificer First Class.'

Sim winked at Caitlin.

'Such a terrible loss to the craft,' the man said with a sigh.

'What happened?' asked Sim, trying not to sound too eager.

'The Mark IV was his masterpiece,' he said, taking one out from the display. 'A consummate example of temporal engineering, it truly is timeless.'

Caitlin had a Mark II. Her grandfather had given it to her as a present for her twelfth birthday. Sim had a Mark IV, which was significantly lighter than the previous model, and it had a torch, but beyond that she'd never given it a second thought. It certainly never occurred to her that someone had devoted their life to creating it.

'Sergeant disappeared after it was finished, and many thought he'd retired—when he surfaced three years later he was a broken man.'

'What happened?' asked Caitlin.

The assayer's eyes narrowed slightly. 'Where exactly did you say you found this mark? It's usually concealed within the inner workings of the device, not something you should be able to see.'

'Her uncle collects them,' blurted Sim, trying to sound convincing and failing.

'Really?' the old man said suspiciously. 'What's his name — I know most of the horologists.'

'Westinghouse,' said Caitlin. 'Rufius Westinghouse. He's a Watchman.'

The man looked puzzled. 'The name is familiar, and I seem to remember something about an early patent. One moment,' he said, wandering off into the back office.

Sim pulled Caitlin to one side. 'We should go,' he whispered.

'I know, he's getting suspicious.'

'No. That inspector turned up with Eddington yesterday asking about an engineer by the name of Sergeant. We ran a search on his timeline. There was something weird about it.'

'Weird how?'

'He'd been murdered,' said Sim, drawing a line across his neck with a finger. 'His line had been terminated at least ten years before its time. Like the old man said, Sergeant had this glittering career, all commendations and promotions, and then there's a sudden redacted part, locked behind all kinds of security. Eddington managed to find a reference to Project Osirion, but no detail. When Sergeant finally resurfaces he took a menial job as second draughtsman on the tachyon upgrade team.'

The old man came out of the back with a large leather bound volume and placed it on the counter. There was a diagram of an antique looking tachyon with a guild stamp in the bottom-right hand corner.

'I knew the name was familiar!' He pointed to a list of names above the stamp. 'Rufius Westinghouse is listed among the creators of the Mark I — I don't suppose you could arrange a meeting could you?'

53

THE MORNING AFTER

Kaori had slept late.

The morning sun was streaming through the half-closed curtains and Schrödinger was sprawled across the bottom of the bed cleaning himself, something that he was taking a great deal of pleasure in doing noisily.

There was a moment, as she surfaced from the dream state, when she assumed that Sabien was still there. Her body ached, and she could still feel the sensation of his mouth on her neck, his strong hands on her hips.

She turned over, pulling the sheets with her and disrupting the cat's routine. He growled and pawed at her hidden feet beneath the covers. She could still smell his cologne on the pillows and she buried her face in it, breathing him in.

It hadn't been planned. After breakfast they had intended to go their separate ways, but she was beginning to enjoy his company and she didn't feel like going home. He tried to make some excuse about having work to do, when she remembered it was Dangerfield's memorial later that day, and she wanted to show him some of his work.

He was interested, she could see it in his eyes. She'd caught him studying her body more than once.

The Natural History Museum was closing as Kaori and Sabien walked in. The visitors were filing out past the large diplodocus skeleton that stood serenely in the central hall.

'Half-day closing,' snapped one of the uniformed guards, stepping in front of them.

'Tempus Fugit,' replied Kaori, pulling her sleeve up to reveal the Ouroboros tattoo — the snake eating its tail.

He nodded and stepped aside to let them pass.

'Dangerfield helped Owen convince the board of trustees to build this place,' she explained, 'and he worked closely with the architect, Waterhouse, to incorporate some rather interesting hidden features.' She nodded to the terracotta casts that adorned the Romanesque pillars. Sabien didn't notice at first, but as he studied the sculpted creatures more carefully he saw a series of very unusual beasts.

'Richard Owen wasn't a big fan of Darwin's theory of evolution, so he insisted that the extinct species were kept apart from the living ones in different wings of the building. What I wanted to show you is in the East Wing.'

She walked through an ornamental arch and up to a small cabinet with a dried out specimen labelled: 'The Mermaid. Fiji Islands, Dr. J. Griffin, British Lyceum of Natural History'.

It looked like the shrivelled tail of a fish skilfully joined to the desiccated head and torso of a monkey.

'No one said Dangerfield didn't have a sense of humour,' she said, tapping the glass. 'Follow me.'

She touched the brass plaque and disappeared.

The exhibits were some of the strangest creatures Sabien had ever seen — even in his worst nightmares. The gallery was an eclectic collection of creatures that the xenobiologysts had captured over the years, each one preserved, labelled, and put on display in tall glass cabinets.

A motley group of black-robed scientists were wandering between the specimens, consoling each other and looking generally unhappy.

Kaori shook a few hands, patted a couple of weeping colleagues on the shoulder and hugged one woman who looked like she'd been crying for two days straight.

'His secretary,' she explained, 'been with him for over thirty years.'

'What is this place?'

'He called it "The Department of the Unknown". A holotype of every creature that Dangerfield ever studied. There are well over four hundred, but there's one in particular I want to show you.'

Sabien had to admit he was impressed, and there were some vicious-looking monsters. One was the size of an elephant except with a terrible array of serrated horns where the trunk should have been.

He followed her through the maze of displays, catching a waiter along the way and grabbing himself a single malt whisky — a particular favourite of Dangerfield's apparently.

She stopped beside a cabinet surrounded by a small group of mourners and an elegant lady dressed in white.

'The first Strzyga ever captured,' the woman intoned, 'and none of us will forget the day he dragged it into my kitchen.'

Everyone laughed.

'He leaves a great legacy,' she said, waving her hand around the room. 'We are all the safer because of him!' She held her glass aloft, and the onlookers followed suit. 'To Daniel Malerant Dangerfield, a true man of science!'

'A man of science,' they intoned as one.

Sabien raised his glass with Kaori, who had a tear running down one cheek.

'Who's the lady?' he whispered.

'Alixia De Freis,' Kaori replied, the faint smell of scotch on her breath. 'She's a legend. Favourite to take his position.'

Sabien knew the name, and had worked with her husband on a case. The Makepiece girl was living with them.

Kaori knocked back the rest of her drink and picked up another.

'Do you want to see the Monument?'

He nodded, not knowing what the monument was, but the whisky was good and there seem to be no end to its supply.

At the very end of the gallery was a door to another room. A vast bronze sculpture dominated the space, which depicted the defence of a breach: terrifying creatures clawing their way out of the aperture as a small group of Dreadnoughts prepared to hold them back. The walls were covered in rolls of honour. The names of every member of the Order lost in the course of their duty — it didn't take long for Sabien to find Maddox. Kaori was staring at the freshly painted name of Dangerfield on a half-empty panel.

'Do you know someone who died?' she asked, wiping her eyes with her sleeve.

'A few,' he replied. 'I never knew this was here.'

'Dangerfield created it after the Great Breach,' she said, pointing to one wall that was dedicated to that event. Sabien estimated there were over a hundred names.

'What was he like?'

She stared at him with big, watery eyes. 'He was a good man, a great one, in fact. This wasn't how it was supposed to end.' Her lip began to tremble.

Then why would someone kill him? Sabien thought to himself.

'Let's get another drink,' he said, putting his hand on her shoulder.

Kaori got up slowly, collecting her underwear off the floor. Schrödinger watched her tidying up as he continued to preen himself.

'And you can stop with the judgemental act!' she said, putting on her kimono. The cat rolled off the bed and followed her downstairs for breakfast.

The old fire station had been converted to act as both an apartment and a laboratory. Framed sketches of her discoveries were displayed along the bare brick walls. She'd found more than a hundred species, and drawn each one by hand.

To Kaori they were magical creatures full of mystery and surprises. No two were alike, and that fascinated her. During her training she'd spent many hours pouring over Dangerfield's bestiaries, hoping to be the first to find some commonality between them — the mythical 'Golden Gene', but each one of them was different, completely unique and beautiful — at least in her eyes.

She learned so much from Dangerfield, and his loss had left a gaping hole in her life, let alone in the department. The man had single-handedly created the field of Xenobiology, and without him there would be no defence against the maelstrom, nothing to help hold back the malevolent forces that existed beyond the chronosphere.

Pouring herself a green tea, she took one of their team photos off the fridge. It was from a Christmas party two years ago. They were all beaming, mostly because they were drunk — everyone was celebrating a major breakthrough in non-corporeal containment, something she'd helped to design.

They were good times, the kind that reminded her why she chose this field. She would liked to have gone on like that forever, but nothing ever did. Two weeks after the photograph was taken she'd had the accident, and then everything changed.

It was a routine transfer. A xenoform had been captured by a Dreadnought team back in the eleventh and her team were called in to take it away.

The usual protocols were observed and the non-corporeal brought back to the lab, but someone had forgotten to lock down the other cells. The new specimen seemed to disturb the others in ways no one could have expected — they broke loose, and as the department went into lock down, she was left on the wrong side of the door.

The temperature reduced automatically as they had designed it to do, and she would have died if it weren't for Ophelia.

Dangerfield had helped her through the transition, bringing her back from the brink — three months inside a hyperbaric chamber with nothing but his voice for company.

54

SUPERINTENDENT

[New York. Date: May 26th 11.930]

The superintendent's office was on the twentieth floor of the Ministry of Justice. Sabien had only ever been higher than the tenth once before. The Protectorate was the epitome of a hierarchical organisation: each grade of officer class had their place on the relevant floor. You literally started at the ground floor and worked your way up.

The ministry was located in a time loop of the Chrysler building on 42nd and Lexington. It followed the Art Deco school of design and was the tallest building of its age. The superintendent of homicide, Tobias Gregson, was a passionate fan of architecture.

Sabien looked at the gold-rimmed buttons as he rode the car up to the twentieth. He'd heard rumours of an exclusive club on the seventy-seventh floor, one that the elite members were given a special elevator key to access.

Homicide was located between floors five and twenty;

above that it got more political. The ministry of internal affairs, 'Stasi', as he called them, had the best part of twenty-one to fifty, and beyond that it was departments with names ending with Xs or no names at all.

The Stasi were the guys that gave the Protectorate a bad name. The ones that people whispered about in dark corners in bars, the ones that turned up in the middle of the night and took you away. Sabien named them after the state intelligence agency of post war East Germany — and he hated them.

Sabien liked to think of himself as a regular cop — upholding the law and protecting the people — but the Protectorate was a political organisation and he didn't do well at diplomacy. Which is why, after twenty years, he was still only Inspector tenth-grade, and he liked it that way.

What he didn't like was being called up to the twentieth, especially when the order had been delivered in person. No telex or note, just a direct order from one of the superintendent's personal assistants.

She stood next to him in the elevator, staring straight ahead with a blank expression and no attempt at small talk. The uniform she wore was tight-fitting and accentuated the curves of her hips. Sabien studied the lines on the back of her stockings all the way down to the non-standard heels she was wearing, and wondered what exactly she'd had done to get a job in the Super's office.

'Twenty,' an electronic voice chimed as the car slowed to a stop.

The doors slid back gracefully and they stepped out onto the most luxurious carpet Sabien had ever seen.

'Wait here,' she ordered when they reached the outer doors of the Superintendent's office.

He did as he was told and sat down in one of the plush leather Chesterfield sofas. She disappeared through the double doors.

The walls of the waiting area were panelled in wood and decorated with scenes from famous battles. Gregson saw himself as something of a master tactician, and was known for quoting lines from some of the ancient generals, like Alexander the Great.

This was the second time Sabien had been called up to the office; the first was after the fiasco with the ripper and Maddox. That time it was a commendation for bravery, going above and beyond the call of duty, and all the BS that went with it. Gregson wasn't interested in the details, just results. Six dead women was a stain on the reputation of the force, but losing one of your own was unforgivable. Sabien wanted answers, but they gave him a medal instead, and moved him to the tenth. Maddox would've been impressed, if only they'd allowed him to go back and save her.

'I've been hearing good things about you, Inspector,' said the Superintendent from the other side of his grand desk. 'Chief Inspector Avery thinks it may be time for you to consider a move up into internal affairs.'

Sabien thought of that as more like a punishment, but kept his mouth shut. If his commander was trying to shift him upstairs he would've told him himself.

'I noticed from your last report that you're making some progress with this murder case. Terrible business, especially Doctor Dangerfield.'

'Yes, Sir.'

'This… ' — he looked at his notes — 'Chimæra. Do you really believe it has some kind of motive.'

'The markings seem to signify a motive.'

The superintendent's eye twitched. It was a subtle tic, but Sabien could tell this wasn't what the old man wanted to hear. The broken blood vessels in his cheeks were a sure sign that the man had high blood pressure and there was a certain pallor to his skin that indicated other complications.

'I think it's very unlikely that a creature such as the one Dr Shika describes would have any grand design. Surely it's just a case of hunting it down and killing the bloody thing before it does any more dama—'

'I believe the creature is merely a weapon,' Sabien interrupted. 'Someone is using it to take revenge. The victims look random at first, but there's a link.'

'Yes,' Gregson said, opening the case report. 'This Belsarus theory of yours — bit of a leap isn't it? Not trying to tell you how to do your job of course, but the man was a lunatic and a laughing stock. I'd be very careful building probable cause around the likes of Johannes Belsarus.'

Sabien could tell from the man's tone that this was a warning. There was some line that he'd crossed, and something he'd done had triggered an alarm that Gregson had been told to fix.

He pushed the report back across his desk. 'So, no more nonsense about this bloody Codex Arcanuum. Are we clear?'

Sabien nodded, then collected the report and turned to leave.

'One other thing, Inspector. The girl, Makepiece… it would be wise to keep an eye on her. The chaps on the sixtieth tell me she's been busy doing some digging of her own, so probably best if you had a quiet word.'

After Sabien had gone, a Protectorate guard stepped out of the shadows.

'You did well, superintendent,' the man's voice hissed as he took off the face plate.

'Colonel Jaeger,' replied Gregson, snapping to attention.

'At ease soldier, no need to stand on ceremony.'

The superintendent relaxed slightly. 'I'm not sure how long I can keep him away from the truth.'

Jaeger smiled, and a scar ran through his eye and down his cheek distorting the side of his face.

'A few more days will be all I need. Once the investiture is over they won't be able to stop me.'

The colonel had been his commanding officer in the old days, before Gregson had joined the Protectorate. The man had saved his life on more than one occasion, and they all bore the scars of battles they'd fought against the maelstrom.

Soon, he would be the commander-in-chief of the Dreadnoughts, and if anyone could end the constant threat that the storm-kin posed, it would be him. There would be no more liberal-minded do-gooders like the Xenos trying to save them — Jaeger would wipe every single last one of them out of existence.

'Do you have copies of the reports?' he asked, holding out a gloved hand.

Gregson handed over Sabien's case notes. He knew better than to refuse him; the man was about to become one of the most powerful members of the Order.

'Thank you,' Jaeger said, strapping the mask back over his face.

'Do yourself a favour, Gregson,' he added, his voice muffled by the filters. 'Put someone else on the Makepiece girl — she's asking all the wrong questions and I'm not convinced Sabien is quite as dependable as you think.'

'He's no lover of the Xeno department,' Gregson scoffed. 'He's every reason to hate them.'

'I wouldn't be so sure. Dr Shika seems to have had quite an effect on him.'

Jaeger moved the dials on his tachyon and disappeared. Gregson let out a sigh of relief and slumped down in his chair. Reaching for one of the lower drawers in his desk he pulled out a bottle of whisky, poured himself a large glass and raised it up.

'Here's to you Marcus, wherever the hell you are.'

55

THIRD VOICE

Caitlin stood in the usual place in the front garden, staring through the window into the warm glow of the study. There was a fire in the hearth and the lamps were low. The clock above the fireplace told her it was past midnight, and her younger self would be fast asleep in her bedroom on the second floor.

The townhouse had belonged to her grandfather, on her mother's side. His duties as a grandmaster were such that he never spent any time there and had given the house to her parents when Caitlin was born.

In a few minutes it would start raining. She stepped to one side of the bay to shelter under the eaves, putting her deep into shadow.

A couple walked past right on cue. The lady's chuckle always made Caitlin smile. Whatever it was that her boyfriend had whispered in her ear was lost, but her response was more than enough of a sign that they were in love.

She braced herself for the shouting; it was less than a minute away now. There were times when she'd imagined that there were three voices, that she'd convinced herself her parents were arguing with someone else. It was so unlike them to raise their voices at each other — it seemed the only logical reason.

'You can't expect us to believe that!' came the booming voice of her father.

'No. I won't do it. There has to be another way!' protested her mother. 'There has to be another way. I won't leave her.'

'It's not fair. She's only ten!'

And so it went on for over an hour. Caitlin had never made it through more than the first ten minutes — it was too painful to repeat. She could still remember sitting on the stairs shivering in her cotton nightdress, listening to her parents argue over her death. It was traumatic enough the first time.

But tonight, something made her go back to the start.

'You can't expect us to believe that!'

She paused time using the technique Rufius had taught her. In reality she was looping on the same millisecond, but it gave the effect of freezing time; the raindrops hung in mid-air while she considered what her father had said. 'Us' was a strange thing to say to your wife; it was something you used in the presence of another. She'd never noticed it before, a subtle phrasing that made all the difference.

Somebody else had been in the house that night. They must have arrived after she'd gone to bed. They were the ones who had brought the bad news.

Lyra was deep in a trance-like meditation, sitting on Rufius' bed with her pale fingers pressed against his temple.

Caitlin stepped back into the timeline, hoping that she wouldn't have noticed the momentary disappearance.

'Where've you been?' Lyra whispered without opening her eyes.

'Needed to check something,' Caitlin replied, knowing Lyra would see through any lie. That was the trouble with seers — they were impossible to beguile. It was a type of autism, seeing the truth in your words before you even spoke them — which had made for some very awkward conversations.

'How is he?' Caitlin asked, kissing the old man on the forehead.

Lyra opened her eyes. 'He's not there. I mean the body is, but the spirit is somewhere else. Not sure quite how to explain it.'

'I think I know what you mean.'

'I can't do anything for him,' Lyra said and sighed, taking her hands back and rubbing them. 'Wherever he is — we need to remind him where he belongs.'

Caitlin knew she had to find Henery Sergeant, for Rufius' sake. He would hold the answer to the accident, and be able to explain more about what his device had done to her parents.

'We need to talk to the engineer, find out what happened.'

'But didn't Sim say he'd been murdered?'

Caitlin nodded, biting her lip. 'Which means the Protectorate will already be monitoring his timeline.'

'Sabien's bound to know about it.'

Caitlin didn't trust the inspector, especially after he'd accused her of being involved in Zillers' murder.

'He won't know the details about Project Osirion.'

'Then perhaps you should tell him,' Lyra suggested.

'Why would I want to do that?'

Lyra rolled her eyes. 'Maybe because he's Protectorate and he can get access to places you can't?'

Caitlin racked her brains for another way, but nothing came to mind.

56

JAEGER

Jaeger stared at the four reports spread out across his desk and took a slow sip of wine.

The names were like phantoms from his past: Zillers, Sergeant, and Dangerfield. All people he'd spent a long time trying to forget, and with the exception of the linear woman, they all shared a terrible secret — one that he'd tried very hard to bury.

Jaeger couldn't shake the feeling that someone was trying to ruin his career. Years of hard work and political lobbying was finally about to pay off: his ascendancy to commander of the Dreadnoughts was a certainty, or at least it had been until he received these reports.

There was too much at stake to hope these murders wouldn't find their way back to him. He'd made some very influential friends on his climb through the ranks — ones that should be able to make issues like this disappear. The last thing he needed right now was Chief Inquisitor Eckhart and her hounds at the Protectorate starting an internal investigation.

Jaeger picked up the photograph of the dead woman and looked at the symbol closely.

'Gateway,' he translated aloud, before draining the rest of the glass. 'Belsarus, you damned fool.'

57

TIMELINE

Sabien had pinned all of his case notes onto the wall. Creating a physical timeline of events always helped him to visualise the movements of the perpetrator, helping him to find the motive.

There was no obvious pattern to their murders, other than the way they died. The pathologist reports said the bruising of their skulls and the massive internal damage was caused by immensely strong hands — ones with claws.

Kaori had printed out an image of the chimæra which he'd pinned in the centre, surrounding it with the four symbols of the murders, like a clock face, each one a quarter of an hour from the other.

Delawney, the 'Gateway', was first, followed by Zillers the 'Forger', Sergeant the 'Toolmaker', and Dangerfield the 'Jailer'.

Connecting Zillers, Delawney and Dangerfield were thin red lines that traced back to a woodcut illustration of Belsarus — it was the closest thing he had to a common thread, except the only problem was it didn't work for Sergeant, and that frustrated Sabien.

Johannes Belsarus wasn't a difficult man to track down. His experiments were all in the public domain, every one a humiliating failure that reinforced the perception of him as a hare-brained inventor obsessed with going into the future. After the last event at the Royal Society, he was never heard from again — except for the Codex Arcanuum, which was only published after his disappearance.

The phone on his desk rang.

'A Miss Makepiece to see you, sir,' said Parks, the desk sergeant, using a condescending tone which implied he was doing something against his better judgement.

Sabien paused before answering. After the warning from the superintendent, he'd been planning to interview her again. The fact that he'd mentioned her at all was intriguing — she was a person of interest, and he needed to know why.

'Send her up.'

'You're missing something,' Caitlin said, studying the wall.

'Really, Miss Makepiece, and what would that be?' Sabien replied dryly.

She took off her overcoat and threw it over the back of the chair. Rain water began to pool on the wooden floor beneath it and Sabien had to restrain himself from clearing it up.

'The Toolmaker,' she began, pointing at Sergeant's symbol. 'He's not directly connected to any of them.'

'I know that,' Sabien stated.

'But indirectly he was involved with Zillers, and my parents.'

'What have your parents got to do with it?'

She turned towards him, anger flashing in her eyes. 'Let me finish and you'll find out.'

He raised his hands in a mock surrender.

Chimæra

She took a pen from his desk and went over to the notes. 'Zillers was called the forger. I've found out why...' She paused for dramatic effect.

'Because he falsified a record.'

'You knew that?'

'He worked in the records department, so it wasn't hard to guess he'd been pressured to change a document or two — especially with a sick wife.'

'Ah, but do you know which record?'

'He had access to millions and I have limited resources, but I've a feeling you're about to tell me.'

She scribbled the names of her parents onto an index card and pinned it between the symbols of Zillers and Sergeant, completely ruining the compass-like symmetry in the process.

'Zillers hid a record that linked my parents to something that Sergeant had worked on — a kind of maelstrom defence system.'

He had to admit he was impressed. She'd found a link that would've taken his small team a year to unearth. Sabien was beginning to suspect that the warning from Gregson was more about covering his own arse than for her safety.

'Go on,' he said, sitting down by his desk. 'You have my undivided attention.'

Caitlin told him about the storage facility and the breach at the Osirion temple. She left out what happened to Rufius; it was still too painful to talk about.

When she finished, there were more notes on his board, and more unanswered questions.

Sabien stared at the wall, tapping his pencil against the desk. 'I still don't see how this connects Sergeant to Belsarus.'

Caitlin folded her arms. 'Where does Belsarus figure in all this anyway?'

He walked over to the wall. 'Madame Delawney was

found dead in the middle of a ritual with one of his symbols carved into her chest. Dangerfield had collected every one of his books and inventions and Zillers had access to the Codex in the restricted section. It's too much of a coincidence.'

'Just because Zillers had access to it, doesn't mean he used it. That's circumstantial at best.'

Sabien had to agree with her, and he was clutching at straws.

'So the creature's killed four people,' she mused. 'Only two of them have an actual connection and one of them isn't even a member of the Order. It's trying to tell us something, but I can't see what.' As she raised her arm to point at Delawney's symbol her sleeve fell back and revealed the silver bracelet.

Sabien caught her hand. 'That's a Draconian tracer. Did your godfather send you to see me?'

She shook her head. 'No!'

'Then why are you here?'

Caitlin pulled her arm back, her eyes full of fire. 'Because the nearest thing I have to a parent is lying in a hospital and Sergeant's contraption put him there. So I was hoping you might be able to help me.'

Sabien's expression hardened. 'This is an official enquiry, Ms Makepiece. Thank you for your concern, but I believe it's time you left.'

'Wait, what about Rufius?' Caitlin complained as Sabien gave her back her coat and walked her forcibly to his office door.

'He should have left it to the experts. I hope he makes a full recovery. Good day.'

58

CODEX

[Anathaeum]

'Lyra this is really important!' Caitlin pleaded.

'Why should I? If I tell you where it is you're going to end up trying to go in there.'

'Why didn't you tell me about it before?'

Lyra looked at her with exasperation. 'You're always the one lecturing me on how it's a load of spooky nonsense. Why on earth would I tell you about it?'

'Because Sabien believes the murders have something to do with Belsarus' books.'

'So why isn't he helping you?'

Caitlin scowled and held up her wrist. 'He freaked out when he saw my tracer. He went all paranoid, like I was setting him up.'

Lyra touched the silver band. 'Yeah, I've heard that can be used for surveillance.'

'Really?' The thought of her godfather spying on her made her want to rip it off.

'But I guess you'd know by now if he was. So which book exactly?'

'I don't know? How many did he write?'

Lyra raised her hands and began to count on her fingers. 'Four about his theories on travelling into the future, three on the mechanics of magnetism, two on astrological anomalies, and of course the *Codex Arcanuum* — the book of shadows.'

'Do any of them involve gateways?' Caitlin asked.

'I'm not an expert! You should speak to Doctor Dangerfield.'

'He's dead.'

Lyra's eyes widened a little. 'There are hundreds of references to portals and gateways in his work. He was constantly looking for a way out of this timeline. His obsession with mirrors drove him mad.'

'Mirrors?'

'Yes, like the one in that old lady's house. The one Kaori's cat took me to the other day. There was still a weak aura around it when I touched it.'

'And you never thought to mention it?'

Lyra shrugged. 'Haven't seen that much of you lately, sorry.'

For a moment Caitlin looked mildly annoyed, and then she had a thought. 'Lyra do you know where to find a copy of the *Codex Arcanum*?'

Lyra nodded. 'Of course, silly. There's one right here in the library, although it's not in its proper place.'

The book of shadows was wedged in between the collected works of Nicolaus Copernicus and Codex Incalcus — a mathematical treatise on the impossibility of PI. It took Lyra over an hour to remember where exactly it was and included three dead-ends, which did nothing to improve Caitlin's mood.

Lyra pulled the old, leather-bound book down from the second shelf and handed it to Caitlin with a look of self-congratulation.

Caitlin laid it open on the nearest reading desk and stood in awe of the decorative frontispiece — the engraving was a work of art. There was an ornate mirror in the centre of the page, split horizontally to show two worlds: day and night, with a man holding a sphere between the two.

'I heard there were only three of these ever printed,' Lyra said, admiring the book. 'How did you think it ended up here?'

'Misfiled,' Caitlin replied, looking at the spine. 'The indexing is pre-Mayerstein, so I'm guessing they just stuck it under miscellaneous. How the hell did you find it?'

'It felt different to the others.'

'Different how?'

'Like it was vibrating.'

Caitlin ran her finger across the soft vellum, wondering how many others had touched the paper. There was no time-line, no past, only the slight tremor of something beyond her reach.

'No better place to hide it really, if you think about,' observed Lyra, looking at the thousands of books around them.

'So where does it mention the gateway?'

Caitlin was flicking through the long table of contents, which seemed to extend to twenty pages. Each entry was hand-written and carefully labelled in a beautiful copperplate.

'The frequency of reflection,' Lyra read aloud, tapping her finger on the line of script.

As Caitlin turned through the pages, Lyra came around to stand next to her.

There was a set of arcane symbols sitting in the middle of the page, surrounded by the tiniest writing they had ever seen.

'It's some kind of magical writing system,' said Caitlin. She leaned in closer, her eyes narrowing on the minute text. 'It's in Latin, and the symbols are astrological I think. We need to go back to the mirror.'

Lyra picked up the book. 'Belsarus coded them for a reason,' she warned her. 'These are very powerful metaphysical forces you're dealing with. He doesn't want just anyone taking the book and using them.'

'I need some answers,' Caitlin insisted, 'and this may be the only way to get them.'

59

CAT

'I need to borrow your cat,' Sabien said, walking into Kaori's lab.

'Hello to you too,' Kaori replied. 'How's the hunt for the Chimæra?'

There was a tension between them, unanswered questions about the previous night lurking dangerously unsaid below the surface of their conversation.

'Slowly, since the Xeno department got involved, but Caitlin Makepiece came to see me today with some important information.'

Kaori raised one eyebrow. 'The redhead?'

'The seventeen-year-old witness,' he reminded her.

'And now you want my cat.'

He nodded. 'I need a tracker.'

Schrödinger lay at her feet licking one of its paws and washing his ear. She bent down and rubbed his muzzle. 'I don't think he's up to it.'

'Don't play games.'

She chuckled. 'Says the man that left before I woke up.'

Sabien's expression hardened, 'I'm not a morning person.'

'No, I worked that out on my own.'

'So can I have the cat?'

She stood up and went over to grab his collar and leash. 'You get us both… we come as a package. Where exactly are we going?'

Sabien seemed to consider the idea for a moment before deciding it was probably better not to force the issue.

'Back to Madam Delawney's — it's the mirror. There's a gateway to the shadow dimension through the mirror.'

Kaori thought back to how Schrödinger had traced the creature's trail to the mirror. The way he had reacted to the reflection had made her uneasy; she'd never seen him scared of anything.

'And you know that how?'

'Caitlin found another one of Belsarus' codices. She's actually gone through Delawney's mirror.'

60

SHADOW

Caitlin shivered as she looked back at the silvery rectangle hanging in mid-air. She could still feel the numbing sensation from stepping through the surface of the mirror — as though every molecule in her body was vibrating at a different frequency.

The twilight world beyond the mirror was a dark and brooding place, reminding her of something from a medieval fairy tale. Narrow cobbled streets wound between tall gothic buildings, lit by flickering gas lamps that cast weak spheres of pale yellow light.

The air smelled of neglect, like the inside of some old shed full of forgotten things that had dried and crumbled where they sat. It was so cold, she could feel the ice on the stones beneath her feet, and when she walked it felt like she was stepping on glass.

Caitlin had no idea what to do next in this alien world, and there was no sign of the creature or Belsarus. She knew instinctively that the answers were in here somewhere, and that tiny glimmer of hope was all she had to keep the rising fear at bay.

It had taken a while to persuade Lyra to show her the mirror. Her friend was adamant that it would only end badly, but Caitlin prevailed. The creature was using the mirrors somehow, and as she read more of Belsarus' codex she realised he'd discovered some kind of parallel timeline.

'You have to tune it,' Lyra said when they arrived in Madame Delawney's apartment. 'The shadow plane uses a different frequency.'

The mirror was dark, reflecting little of the light in the room. 'So Belsarus worked out the right one?'

Lyra nodded, holding his book tightly to her chest and refusing to let Caitlin near it.

'It's better if you don't know how. The summoning takes practice, and we don't have much time. I will leave the gateway open so you can get back.'

Caitlin nodded, and watched as her friend placed the book on the floor and wrote glyphs in chalk around it.

Lyra leaned forward so her lips were close to the mirror and whispered the incantation, her breath fogging the glass.

The words where like a hypnotic poem, more sounds than anything of meaning. As she listened she could make out different tones building on each other, the sounds overlapping, like waves. Then she saw the book. The cover was pulsating, lines of energy threading through the design, brought to life by Lyra's voice.

Belsarus had built some kind of device into the book itself.

A cold knot formed in her stomach as Caitlin forced herself onward up the hill. Shadows seemed to move behind her, stalking her, but when she turned there was nothing.

'You're seeing things,' she told herself.

A chilling wind swept down the street, rattling the rusting signs hanging above the abandoned shop fronts, whispering through the papery leaves on the desiccated trees.

Lyra had told Caitlin that Belsarus believed time moved at a different speed in the shadow plane. That he'd aged ten times faster than in the continuum. She looked up into the clear night sky and saw the same stars burning brightly — *other peoples suns*, she thought. Clouds scudded across them, too fast to block out their light, but no sunrise came — it was as though day had been forgotten.

'You do not belong here,' said a hollow voice.

She turned, expecting to see the creature, but instead found a withered old man.

'Who are you?'

He lifted his head so she could see him better in the pale light.

'Once, a long time ago, I was known as Johannes Belsarus. In this world you may call me "Keeper". They all do.'

'Belsarus, but you —'

'Died?' He laughed hoarsely. 'One version of me perhaps, a reflection.'

Far off, beyond the town, she heard a high-pitched wail, like the screech of a fox, and the old man turned his head towards it.

'Did you hear that?' he asked. 'Sometimes I imagine sounds.'

She nodded.

'Good,' he smiled, and began to walk towards her. 'And also bad. They've filled my world with terrible creatures. The ones that remember who they once were can be reasonable, but many more are not — now come.' He held out a wrinkled, withered hand. 'We have to get you off the street.'

61

MIRRORS

Sabien and Kaori gazed into the front of the blackened mirror.

'So this is definitely the point of entry,' Kaori said, looking at the book that Lyra had left on the floor in front of the mirror. The symbols chalked onto the floorboards around it were still glowing faintly.

'She's a fool,' snapped Sabien. 'There's no logical reason to go in there.'

'Logic doesn't enter into it. She's a daughter looking for her parents, and this is the only lead she's had in years.'

He stared at the mirror. 'Will Schrödinger go in there?'

The cat's hackles were raised, growling at its own reflection. 'I'm not sure. He's scared of something. I've never seen him like this.'

It was like staring into a dark painting of a town in the middle of the night. Except this picture was moving; clouds shifted across the stars, trees swayed on silent winds, and bat-like creatures circled the lamplights.

Sabien reached out to the still shimmering surface of the mirror and felt the cold, as though putting his hand on a window in the middle of winter. Instead of resistance from the glass, the tips of his fingers felt the surface give way and he pushed his hand in further.

Kaori snatched it back. 'What are you doing? You're not seriously just going to go in there? There are a hundred different safety protocols to go through; hazmat suits, breathing apparatus, checks for radiation and environmental toxins — the kind of stuff that stops you getting something fatal?'

'I don't have time for risk assessments. Stay here,' he said, pulling his hand back and stepping through the surface.

Kaori watched in stunned silence as Sabien disappeared into the image, appearing as a much smaller figure in the picture, like some animated character walking off up the street.

Her years of training were telling her not to follow, as there were far too many risks. All of her research had been in the relative safety of the lab. She'd never been that interested in field work, and yet Kaori knew that this was probably going to be her only opportunity. Fear and excitement ran through her body; it was a weird feeling — nearly as strange as the way she had begun to feel about Sabien. There were butterflies in her stomach and the urge to leap through the mirror and join him was becoming hard to resist.

Kaori closed her eyes and took a series of deep breaths, counting to four and back on each exhale. Her pulse slowed and so did the anxiety.

Thinking more clearly, she realised that no one else knew where they were or what they were planning to do. She took out her almanac and wrote a quick note to Bellamy. It was nothing more than their temporal location, and while she waited for his acknowledgement she looked around for some kind of weapon — she couldn't be sure Schrödinger would follow her in.

Delawney had a fascinating collection of ritualistic daggers. Kaori selected the meanest looking one and pushed it through her belt, then took another one for a backup and slipped it inside her boot.

Kneeling down beside her cat, she ruffled the fur under his chin, his eyes narrowing with pleasure.

'So Cat, are you ready for a big adventure?'

The cat twisted its head, allowing her to get behind his ear, and purred loudly.

The mirror image was beginning to fade. Kaori could hardly see Sabien as she took a deep breath and stepped through the mirror, Schrödinger following dutifully behind her.

62

CALIBAN

Belsarus' house was nothing more than a shell; a remnant of a grand mansion, ruined and crumbling in an overgrown estate.

The old man struggled up the stone staircase leading to the main entrance, breathing hard as he paused at the top and looked out over what was left of his lands.

'This used to be the most exquisite garden,' he said with a sigh. 'It took Capability Brown the best part of twenty years to complete.'

Even though a blanket of thorny brambles had reclaimed it, Caitlin could still make out the detail of topiary and the lines of forgotten paths.

'There's even a hidden lake, just over yonder hill.' He pointed with a bony finger into the distance. 'A boy drowned in it once. Can't remember his name, but father wouldn't let us go down there after that. I had a boat called *Prospero*... she's probably still there now.'

The sound of another howl echoed over the fields and Belsarus motioned for them to move inside.

The hall was lit by hundreds of candles, their flames hardly seeming to flicker.

'Stasis lights,' he said, nodding to the candles. 'A little invention on mine.' He hung his cloak on a wooden peg. He was dressed like a fourteenth-century merchant, with a tunic, belt and undershirt that were all threadbare and worn. 'Are you hungry? I'm sorry I never asked your name.'

'Caitlin. Caitlin Makepiece.'

He frowned, repeating her name quietly to himself, as though it were familiar, but yet he couldn't quite recall why.

Belsarus gave up with a shake of his head and closed the front door, escorting her into what was left of the study.

The room was full old books, plans, and models of half-finished contraptions.

'More than a lifetime's work,' he muttered, lowering himself into a chair by the fire. It too had flame but Caitlin felt no heat from it.

'Something's wrong with the entropy in this dimension,' he explained, seeing her interest in the fire. 'Heat seems to dissipate more rapidly here. No idea why, but I can never get warm.'

'What is this place?' Caitlin asked, her voice sounding strangely weak.

'It's my home, or at least the reflection of it. This house has been in my family for generations.'

Caitlin looked up at the holes in the ceiling. The floorboards had rotted away and she could see the sky through the rafters. The walls of the room around them were shored up with a variety of rusting metal bracers that looked likely to fail at any minute.

'How did you find this place? This dimension?'

'Quite by accident, actually.' Belsarus chuckled hoarsely. 'My pursuit of the future had led to so many unsuccessful experiments, but the final failure produced a rather interesting and unexpected result. It's all to do with the oscillation of time, quite simple when you understand the underlying gravimetric frequencies. Although it does have its side effects — I wouldn't stay here too long if I were you.'

Caitlin wasn't sure she wanted to know what it was doing to her right now. There was no way to measure how long she'd been in this dimension, and the passage of time was hard to estimate when there was no sun.

She felt the tracer bracelet shift on her wrist and wondered if her godfather would be able to find her in here. She doubted it was designed to cross into parallel dimensions.

There were uneven footsteps outside the study and the sound of someone dragging something.

'Come in, Caliban,' Belsarus called out. 'She won't hurt you.'

A hideous creature dragged itself into view. Nearly bent double, its arms distorted at strange and irregular angles, his head a bulbous mass of tumour-like growths.

'Keeeeeper,' he moaned. 'Isss food?'

'Yes, my boy,' Belsarus said, patting it like a dog. 'It's feeding time.'

For a horrible moment, Caitlin thought they were referring to her as food, but Belsarus took a small parcel out of his pocket and unwrapped it. The meat smelled rotten and she struggled to hide her disgust as the creature devoured it.

Belsarus caught the look on her face. 'He's quite harmless, as long as he's fed regularly. The problem is keeping the food — it spoils so quickly here, but Caliban doesn't seem to mind.'

The creature was making a terrible mess. His mouth didn't close properly and pieces of his meal kept falling out onto the floor. Small beetle-like insects came out of the skirting and swarmed over them.

'What is he?' she asked quietly.

Belsarus stroked the creature tenderly as it turned its attention to the beetles, catching them with misshapen fingers and swallowing them whole.

'An outcast,' he said, smiling. 'He was my very first patient. The good doctor knew that I would care for him. He was my first Chimæra and still my favourite.'

'There are more like him?' asked Caitlin.

Belsarus beamed with pride. 'Oh, yes. They're all my children: revenants and outcasts — the bastard offspring of the continuum and the maelstrom.'

He stood up slowly and stretched his back.

'I suppose you would like to meet them?'

He led her through the house, passing rooms in various states of disrepair until they reached a series of large, arched windows and walked out onto a veranda overlooking a miniature zoo.

Extending out into the gardens, the square enclosures of iron railings were arranged like a model village. Each intersection was marked with a classical stone fountain of nymphs or fauns.

Caitlin imagined that it would have been quite beautiful in its day, but nature was reclaiming its own: the bars were rusting, and black vines grew between them and into the brickwork.

'My father was a natural philosopher,' explained Belsarus, taking out a large set of keys. 'We were the first to have a tiger, and I can still remember the day it arrived — quite a magnificent beast.'

They walked down the steps into an avenue of cages.

'Did you bring it into this dimension?'

Chimæra

'No, it died many years ago. These pens hold much stranger creatures these days.'

Approaching the first of the cages, Caitlin could smell the creature before she saw it. It had long, leathery wings which it tried and failed to open in the small enclosure. Its beak-like face came close to the bars, screeching at the old man, who took a bucket of rotting fish from Caliban and threw a handful over the bars.

He wiped his hands on a rag that was tied to the pail. 'I call her the Crow, as she was once the most graceful flier, but sadly her wings had to be clipped.'

Caitlin watched the bird-lady devour the fish. She made a retching cough as she ate, as though it pained her to eat.

'What's wrong with her?'

'Oh, they all catch it in the end. Their physiology doesn't adapt well to the temporal frequencies of this dimension.' His eyes filled with tears. 'I've never found a way to heal them.'

Belsarus walked on ahead. Caitlin wanted to give the crow some more food, but when she looked into the bucket she changed her mind. The contents were already crawling with maggots.

Caliban hung back, staring at Caitlin with his pure blue eyes.

'Stay close, as I don't want you wandering off into the lions den, as they say,' warned Belsarus.

She quickened her step. 'Where did they all come from?' she asked, passing more sick and grotesque exhibits.

'They used to bring them every few months. Then for no reason they just stopped. I was never given a reason. I had no choice but to look after them. Couldn't leave them to starve. Ah, here we are.'

Caitlin wondered who 'they' were. They looked like failed

experiments from the Xeno department, but she couldn't understand why someone would want to keep them in here.

'I knew I recognised your family name,' said Belsarus, tapping his head. 'Just takes a while for the brain to catch up these days. Ms Makepiece, I believe this is your uncle — Marcus.'

Standing in the middle of a large enclosure was Caitlin's nightmare — Lyra's Madrigor.

The creature seemed to sense their presence, lifting its head as if scenting the air, and then moved stealthily towards them.

'He's been a naughty boy, lately. Haven't you old chap!' Belsarus banged on the bars with his stick. 'Been out of his cage without permission.'

As it came closer, Caitlin could see there were manacles on its hands and feet, and open scars on his skin where someone had lashed him.

'Marcus?' was all she could manage. Her parents had never spoken about anyone called Marcus, let alone an uncle.

'Yes.' Belsarus motioned to her to look more closely.

Stepping forward, she saw the lip of the hole too late, and fell through into the water-filled pit below.

Caliban slammed the grille down and laughed manically like a hyena.

Belsarus peered down through the bars. 'I'm sorry, my dear, we really don't appreciate uninvited guests. I should mention that he has a particular appetite, but I wouldn't want to spoil his fun. You'll find him an interesting dinner guest.'

The wind carried Caliban's laugh as they walked off into the night.

63

MISSING

Rufius woke with a start and sat bolt upright in the bed, waking Lyra, who nearly jumped out of her skin.

'Caitlin?' he asked, confused and bleary-eyed.

'No, it's Lyra. Lyra De Freis,' she said, taking his hand gently and squeezing it. 'It's good to have you back.'

'Where is Caitlin? I have to tell her.'

'Calm yourself. She's had to go on an errand. I'm sure she won't be long,' Lyra lied, wondering whether now was a good time to tell Rufius what had happened.

'I need to tell her something,' he groaned, before falling back into the pillows. 'She's in danger. The creature is not what it seems.'

His eyes closed as the nurse came running in.

'Out!' she ordered, waving her hands and shooing Lyra from the room.

Lyra tried to protest, but the old nun was having none of it.

64

THE ART OF FORGETTING

The buildings reminded Sabien of a ruined version of Oxford. There were small, narrow streets, archaic old colleges and abandoned museums, but strangely no street names.

It was a dead place, as if life had deserted it. Even the trees were hollow shells that held nothing of any use, their timelines empty or distorted and unstable.

Sabien kept to the shadows, trying to shake the nagging sensation that someone was watching him.

At first he thought Kaori might have disobeyed his orders and followed him in. He was glad she hadn't; having to worry about her would just create more problems — although her cat would've made a useful tracker.

Protecting Caitlin was his primary objective. Once she was safe he could focus on locating the creature, assuming that it hadn't found her already.

He was still trying to decide if she was very brave or incredibly stupid — or maybe both. It had taken a lot of courage to come in here, and in many ways she reminded him of Maddox. The same feisty determination and stubbornness, the kind you couldn't help but admire — but which was ultimately going to lead to trouble.

The dark alleys and gas lamps of the narrow streets reminded Sabien of that night in the backstreets of Whitechapel. Maddox's body was pale and lifeless when he found her, like a marionette whose strings had been cut. He'd wanted to save her, but the Copernicans assured him that someone else would've died in her place and she would never have allowed that.

The horrors he witnessed the day they caught the Xargi had scarred him both mentally and physically. Sabien promised himself that he would never let anything leave him so vulnerable again. He turned the pain of her death into a shield, using it to harden himself against emotional attachments.

Just like he'd done when they found his mother.

She never recovered from the death of his father, no matter what he tried. The police found no reason for his execution, and the lack of knowing had eaten away at her soul until she lost her faith, and without that she had no reason to live.

The priest stood on the doorstep, his face wet with rain as he made his excuses. Sabien could see he was conflicted, but there was no absolution for a suicide, no matter how devout she might have been.

When he went to the Protectorate for advice, Sabien's mentor told him there was nothing that could be done. The timeline was the best outcome for the greater good, no matter what the personal cost, and then he taught him the art of forgetting.

It wasn't easy. At first, the image of his mother's cold, dead eyes staring up at him from her bed, her hands clasped around her rosaries, haunted him. He dragged himself through each day, living most of it in the past. He thought of so many ways to fix it, but none of them would work. There was an art to forgetting, and it began with looking forward, to start living his own life, but part of him knew if he moved on it was like admitting defeat.

It took years, but slowly he forgave himself. Until it happened again — with Halli Maddox.

He hadn't known she was going to volunteer as bait until she turned up looking like a tuppenny tart, flouncing around the office in her usual way. They'd all laughed and joined in — apart from him. He'd argued with her the day before about another case. It was just some random point of procedure, and she'd told him he was being an asshole and stormed off. As he watched her flirting with the junior officers he knew she was doing it to provoke him; there was a look of defiance in her eyes.

Maddox had gone without another word, and they never got to make up. He never got to tell her how much he cared about her.

'Hey, fat noisy bloke behind the tree,' came a familiar voice.

Kaori came running up the middle of the street, her cat loping ahead towards him.

'Did you miss me?'

He tried not to smile, but failed.

'God you're so predictable,' she said, and reached up and

kissed him. 'Next time we're going on a dangerous mission, at least give a girl time to pack a gun or two.'

She offered him one of her daggers, but he declined and pulled open his coat to reveal a small armoury concealed in the lining.

'Wow! You're full of surprises.'

65

THE RACE

Caitlin couldn't move.

Fear seized her muscles, freezing her to the spot, while the creature paced around the centre of the enclosure, testing its chains and shaking its manacles.

She controlled her breathing using the techniques that Rufius had taught her. 'Slow the fear,' he would instruct her calmly as she stood on the edge of a cliff or held her hand in a nest of scorpions. He called it 'desensitisation', but at the time she thought it was more like sadism.

'Slow the fear,' she repeated to herself. 'Let the adrenaline dissipate until you can think clearly.'

Every fibre of her body wanted to run. There was no sign of a fight response — only flight. Slowly, she felt her muscles begin to relax as her heart rate came down.

The monster crouched down onto all fours, its head twisting from side-to-side as it blindly scanned for any sound. The clank of the chains was distracting, and it snapped at them like a dog angry at its own tail.

Caitlin tried to estimate how far the chain would stretch. She couldn't be sure if the creature could reach her.

Animal bones littered the ground, or at least she told herself that's what they were. The enclosure was circular, with high metal railings on all sides. On the opposite side of the round were stone steps leading up to a metal door and some kind of sleeping quarters. It was hanging open and looked sturdy enough to keep him out — if she could reach it.

Her clothes were soaked from the pit and she could feel the cold seeping into her skin. An involuntary shudder ran down her spine and she clamped her jaw hard to stop her teeth chattering.

Think about something else, she told herself.

Belsarus had said it was her uncle, but her parents had never mentioned any siblings. The crazy old man had obviously lied to get her closer to the pit. Whoever it used to be, there was little hope of asking any questions before having her throat ripped out.

The thing had been terribly treated. A lattice of scars across his body showed signs of repeated beatings: bright pink welts of freshly healed skin sat over older scar tissue. Caitlin would have wept for it had she not witnessed what he was capable of. It was clear that Belsarus' mistreatment had obviously driven it mad.

The creature began to feel its way across the floor, flicking aside the whitened bones and dragging the chains quietly across the mud and dust.

Caitlin stood motionless, watching it come closer, inch-by-inch. It was heading off to the right; another metre and she would have enough of a gap to make for the door.

Three more steps and I go, she promised herself, w*hen he reaches that small skull*.

The sounds of bones cracking under the soles of her boots

drove her on, her feet flying across the dirt as she raced for the metal door. It was less than twenty metres, the shortest race that she'd ever had to run, and yet each step seemed to take an eternity.

She heard the chains shifting and then the baleful howl as he turned to follow.

The door was only a few yards away when she felt his breath on the back of her neck.

A claw caught around her ankle and she went down, her head hitting the stone step as everything went black.

66

EDIFICES

Kaori looked up at the bombed-out gothic buildings. 'What was this place?'

'Oxford, I think,' Sabien said, staring up at the crumbling edifices.

Schrödinger appeared out of a doorway on the far side of the street. He was licking his lips.

Kaori called him back to her side. 'Well, at least someone's getting fed.'

'We'll find something,' he said, trying to sound confident.

'Yeah, or we could have planned this a bit better?'

He started walking away. 'We're not going to be in here for much longer.'

'I was going to ask how you were planning to get out. Because, you know, I assumed that you had an exit strategy.'

'We need to find Caitlin,' he growled. 'Then we'll worry about getting out of here.'

They followed her cat through the city, an awkward silence

growing between them as they searched the ruins of the ancient colleges.

Kaori stopped every now and then to examine some plant or dead thing, slowing down their progress.

As she knelt down beside another decaying mammal, Sabien tutted and turned around. 'Do you have to study every damn corpse we come across?'

'I'm a scientist in an unknown environment… what did you expect me to do?'

'We're in a hostile environment,' he reminded her, suddenly sounding every part the Protectorate officer. 'Trying to save a lost girl from leaving in a bodybag.'

She stood up and brushed the dirt off her knees. 'I've discovered over a hundred species, and each one of them taught me something new about their world. They're like books to me, because of the way their environment has shaped them — would you like to know what I've found so far? Or are you so thick-headed that you don't want to hear it?'

He took out a weapon from inside his coat and cocked it. 'This is a Felstock Gunsabre, which can fire five ten-mill rounds a second or slice you in half with a steel blade that has been folded over two hundred times. This is all I need in this situation — this and your cat — everything else is irrelevant.'

She scowled at him. 'What is it about the male psyche that drives them to kill anything they can't eat or screw?'

67

MEMORIES

Caitlin awoke to find herself inside a small, brick chamber. The side of her face felt swollen, and there was a tight, sticky feeling around her eye and down her left cheek.

The creature had shed its chains and was standing over her, stroking her hair.

He didn't kill me, she thought.

The blank face gave no hint as to his intentions, but the gentle caress of the long clawed hand on the side of her head intimated that it wasn't a threat.

'I'm Caitlin,' she stammered. 'Caitlin Makepiece.'

With the benefit of hindsight, it was probably the most ridiculous thing to say, but all she could think of was that Belsarus had said he was her uncle.

The creature's head tilted ever so slightly, like a dog trying to understand what its owner was saying.

His other hand reached up so that he held her head between them and she felt the pressure of thumbs on her temples.

Suddenly she was in his memory, back in her parent's house, the rain clattering on the windows and their voices raised in the kitchen.

But she wasn't sitting on the stairs any more. She was there in the room.

Her mother and father were sitting at the kitchen table with another man: he was fair and wiry, his hair tied back in a pony tail and streaked with grey. His arms were covered in archaic symbols.

He had the same nose as her father, and it was obvious that they were brothers, although there was something about the stranger's eyes that spoke of sadness.

'You have no choice,' he said in a raised voice. 'She won't survive without some kind of intervention.' He pointed to a large temporal chart that was spread out across the table.

'You can't expect us to just abandon her,' her mother protested, tears rolling down her cheeks.

Her father was shaking his head, his cheeks flushed red. 'There has to be another way.'

His brother stood up. 'I've been investigating this for years. Don't you think I've checked every possible alternative? It always ends the same way. Do you think I want my niece to die?'

'But who will look after her, Marcus?' asked her sobbing mother.

'Rufius is a good man. He will teach her how to survive this.' He waved his hand at the branching lines that wove across the chart.

'She can't, Thomas, we can't let her die!'

Her mother shook her head and buried it into her father's shoulder.

Marcus looked directly at Caitlin and smiled, and she realised he was trying to share something with her.

The kitchen twisted away.

The next memory was based at a Draconian military base. Caitlin didn't recognise the surroundings, but there were Dreadnoughts everywhere. They were preparing for a mission, putting on breaching armour and checking their weapons.

Marcus stood amongst a small group of hardy-looking men trading stories and comparing scars and tattoos.

An armoured carrier materialised out of thin air and a high-ranking officer walked down the ramp with a group of Antiquarian scientists in tow. They were each carrying a long black case, and looked extremely nervous in the company of the battle-hardened soldiers.

'Sergeant Makepiece,' barked the commander. 'Your squad has been selected to trial a new preservation system.'

'Sir!' Marcus snapped to attention, as did the men behind him.

Caitlin could read the words 'Jaeger' above the breast pocket of the officer.

The Antiquarians began to unpack the kit from the long cases. They were the brass breastplates she'd seen in the storage facility. Each one came with a backpack and Marcus' men began complaining about the extra weight as the scientists helped them strap the equipment onto their shoulders.

'These are salvation devices,' explained Jaeger. 'An EVAC system for pulling you out of the maelstrom should you find yourself on the wrong side of it.'

Marcus examined the kit. 'Permission to speak freely, Sir.'

Jaeger nodded.

'No disrespect to our guests, but why are we using Antiquarian tech when we have our own artificers?'

'Because this was developed by the same team that

worked on the tachyon Mark IV, and we all know how reliable that is.' The officer held up his hand, exposing the golden watch on his wrist.

Marcus nodded and turned towards Caitlin, his gaze lingering on her before the memory dissipated away like smoke.

Her parents were standing at the edge of the breach. Marcus and his team were fighting monads and swarms of other dark creatures. The distortion in time was spewing out monsters faster than they could be neutralised. Caitlin had never seen so many Draconians in one place; there were literally hundreds of men and women fighting the onslaught from hell.

Something exploded close to her ear, and she turned to see a darkly armoured division of Dreadnoughts carving their way through the creatures towards the swirling aperture.

Marcus and her parents were close to the breach when the Dreadnoughts deployed the second charge. She could tell it was a Hubble invertor by the shape of the explosion, and watched the breach expand like a cancer for a split second before it began to implode, taking everyone and everything close to the event horizon with it.

68

BEASTIARY

Lyra waited until the nurse left and went back in to try and rouse Rufius. Her powers as a healer were strong, but he was a difficult subject. She assumed that he had recovered enough for his consciousness to resurface, but as she explored his mind it seemed as closed off as before.

There were only so many ways in which she could help him. As a seer she could read his timeline and look at his potential futures, but that wasn't always easy in subjects with such complicated histories. His personal timeline looked like a web spun by a drunken spider; there was no logical structure to it. However, she could pick out clusters of activity, points in his past that he had revisited many times, and recognised the familiar pattern of retrograding. Like Caitlin and her parents, these were paths of grieving, lines that led back to painful events — ones that remained unresolved.

Lyra touched on the most recent cluster, teasing the event open carefully so that she could jump out if it turned toxic. He was with Caitlin in a storage facility, rifling through boxes — looking for something. It was a cold, distant place, far from civilisation. The world outside was nothing but snow and ice. Caitlin had frost bite on her fingers, and their breath froze in the air like white smoke.

Caitlin had a piece of metal and was attempting to weave it when Rufius snatched it out of her hands.

Unprepared for what he unlocked, Lyra's body went rigid as the energies of the event were unleashed. She felt the edges of the maelstrom envelope her, the pull of the void as it took her inside into a swirling mass of chaos.

The metal was part of a machine, a device strapped to her chest, but not her chest, a man — someone, not Rufius, but a soldier, and she felt his confusion and despair as the breach disappeared from view.

Darkness — total darkness — surrounded him. Unearthly creatures came out of the endless night, their clawed fingers teasing at his skin. She could feel his fear as in desperation he reached for the device on his chest. There was a flash of blinding light when he hit the dial and then pain, terrible pain, as he was wrenched out of the chaos. His body was ravaged, transformed into something inhuman and no longer his own.

Letting out a long sigh, Lyra broke the connection between them and opened her eyes.

Rufius was staring at her in disbelief.

'You saw it?'

She nodded weakly, her face pale and drained of all colour.

'The creature is one of ours,' the old man whispered.

'More than that,' Lyra said with a look of concern. 'He's Caitlin's uncle.'

69

PARADOX

Belsarus hummed along to the sound of the keys as they jangled against his thigh. He couldn't quite remember the title; something by Bach or Debussy? It had been so long since he'd heard any kind of music that it didn't seem to matter any more.

There were fifty pens in his zoo. He'd lost count of how many children he cared for over the years. Too many, some might say, and 'care' may have been overstating it.

He was their Keeper, there was no better word for it, and now he was setting them free.

There was some part of him that always knew this day would come, when he would have to relinquish his position, when those fools that laughed at his theories would realise what he'd actually discovered and come looking for him.

He could still remember the day that Dangerfield had found him. He was a fellow of the same college, and a man of science, and he had deciphered the codex as only one of a superior intellect would — he'd called it 'inspired'.

The first beast Dangerfield brought to him was an abomination, but the doctor had pleaded its case well. Belsarus could care for it, and after years of isolation and loneliness he would finally have a purpose — he took the beast on, made him his Caliban, and soon there were more.

Shuffling down the long rows of cages, he spoke the names of his creatures as he opened each one of their rusted metal cages. Some were too old and frail to realise they were free and simply lay shivering in their own filth. Others, fuelled by hate and loathing, sprang forward and out into the night, not sparing a moment to look back at the man who had imprisoned them.

She had come, as Marcus had predicted all those years ago. She wore the silver band of a Draconian, and that meant others would follow.

Marcus had been so badly damaged when he arrived, horribly transformed by the accident — the only survivor from his squad. Dangerfield said it was something to do with an experiment. He was a Dreadnought, a soldier, and they made for the worst kind of patients. Belsarus had cause to discipline him so many times, and as the months passed his humanity seemed to recede, leaving nothing but the storm-kin.

Before Marcus lost the ability to speak, they'd had many conversations about his life and the things that he'd seen on his missions. He was a maverick, a Dreadnought who had gone rogue. His commander had been an officer called Jaeger — the one he blamed for his condition. Marcus would rage about the 'bastard' for hours, cursing him and swearing revenge on him if he ever got back to the real world.

But there was something else, his 'secret', he called it, smiling that terrible smile as if taunting his keeper.

'In the void I saw the future,' he began. 'Something is

coming that will end you and everything you hold true. It begins with the girl and ends with the Paradox.'

Belsarus had spent his life trying to travel into the future and Marcus would enrage him by refusing to tell him what it was. He would beat the creature until his skin was raw, and every time Marcus' personality would disappear a little more.

I created the monster, Belsarus thought to himself, and now the girl is here and he has forgotten. There was a subtle irony to the situation.

70

MONSTERS

The first shot resounded across the street like a thunderclap. Kaori had heard gunfire before, but the tomb-like stillness of the place amplified it a hundredfold.

'Run. Make for the church,' Sabien shouted, lowering his gun.

Her ears were ringing as she sprinted towards the cathedral, and pain lanced through her ribs as she ran. The creature that attacked her lay dead. Schrödinger had killed it, but its talons had cut deep into her side while her stupid analytical brain was trying to classify it.

More shots rang out, each one sounding like they'd hit their target.

She slowed down as she neared the church, hearing his footsteps close behind her. Sabien kicked open the old wooden door and pushed her inside.

'There are too many of them,' he said, breathing hard.

She held out her hand and was shocked to see it was covered in blood. 'Give me a gun,' she demanded.

He took out a pistol and handed it to her. 'What happened to your scientific principles?'

Kaori took the weapon, ejected the magazine and expertly reloaded and cocked it. Sabien raised an eyebrow.

'Dad was a GI, remember. I spent a lot of time on an army base before he went home.'

He checked his own ammunition and winced. 'Not enough. We need a better plan.'

'Finally!' she said, and laughed, then winced from the pain.

'Do you have anything useful to add?' he asked, jamming a large wooden joist under the handle of the door.

'This place is tactically flawed,' she observed. 'We need to get somewhere with a lower number of approaches and a clear line of sight.'

'Like the crypt?' he said, pointing towards the back of the church.

She shrugged. 'As long as the dead aren't about to rise.'

71

MARKINGS

The howls of rampaging monsters outside brought Caitlin back to reality.

Rubbing her temples, she looked around the room. There was no sign of Marcus; he'd left her alone and unhurt — at least physically. But mentally she was a wreck. He'd given her too much to deal with, revealing parts of his past that gave her nothing more than half the story, and creating a hundred new questions to answer.

Something had happened to him when he came back from the maelstrom. The EVAC device had misfired, and it had changed him, but Caitlin couldn't tell if her parents had suffered a similar fate. She hated the idea that the maelstrom might have mutated them — turning them into monsters.

At least she wasn't afraid of him any more. The sharing of his memories meant that he was still in there somewhere, trapped within that terrible form.

The howling started again. A chorus of primal screams that could only mean the monsters had gotten loose and taken over their zoo — Belsarus had lost control.

Caitlin got up from the chair and went over to the door.

Chimæra

It was made from a heavy iron plate, the kind that they used in nuclear bunkers, and it had been locked from the outside. Marcus had shut her in — she assumed for her safety.

Letting her fingers explore the surface of the door, she searched for a timeline to work with. All she uncovered were countless nights of desperate scraping as Marcus etched the metal with his new claws.

Caitlin stood back and studied the surface in more detail. The marks weren't all random. Amongst the frustrated slashes were symbols, archaic forms of writing she had never seen outside of Dorrowkind's office.

Looking around the dirty walls of his prison, she found the brickwork was covered in thousands of carefully carved pictograms.

'The forger,' she said to herself when she found the familiar symbol. Next to it were a few indecipherable glyphs, and then she saw the 'Toolmaker' and the 'Jailer'.

Lines ran between them and others, a kind of map of everyone that had done him wrong and the rationale for a whole suite of revenge.

At the centre of his plan was a symbol that Caitlin had to study for a long while before she finally got it.

It was inverted, which threw her for a while, but it was the Babylonian sign for 'Commander'.

Caitlin knew then that there was still one more murder to come.

72

COMMANDER

Jaeger read the Copernican memo on Sabien for the third time. He had gone off the grid, as had the Makepiece girl and the Xeno specialist. There were no active connections between their almanacs or tachyons. They had left the continuum. Frustrated, he tore the report in two and dropped it into the fire.

'One more day,' he said to the flames. 'One more day and it's over.'

Watching the paper blacken, Jaeger wished that part of his past could be so easily eradicated. It was a curse he couldn't lift.

Having the worst breach in the Order's history occur on his watch had been bad enough, but to multiply that with the catastrophic failure of their salvation systems, ones that he'd commissioned, was unforgivable. He had sent a lot of good Draconians to their deaths that day, and an even worse fate for those that survived.

He could still see their twisted bodies when he closed his eyes; hear their terrible screams as the maelstrom disfigured

Chimæra

them. They were his men, and he'd sent them into hell thinking they had a chance, a false hope.

The EVAC device was flawed, though no one ever knew why. Project Osirion was cancelled and the victims of the 'accident' were shipped off to some secret medical facility. Jaeger never knew where; that was left to the Director of Xenobiology, Dangerfield, who was keen to examine this new hybrid, or 'Chimæra', as he called them. It had taken Gregson a while to persuade him that the Xeno department were best able to care for his men and the terrible creatures they were becoming.

That was the last time he saw Marcus Makepiece, or what was left of him. One of his best officers transformed into a gruesomely deformed storm-kin. Jaeger had wanted them euthanised, but Dangerfield said that they could make a valuable contribution to science.

Jaeger stared at himself in the mirror. He had aged badly, and the tired, grey face that glared back at him was not filled with satisfaction or contentment. He was about to take the position he had spent his entire career working towards, and yet the old soldier that stood framed in the gilded reflection looked as if the worries of the world were sitting on his shoulders.

There was a knock on the door and his assistant, Donnelly, entered.

'They're ready for you, Sir.'

The high council was the last hurdle in his journey: formed of the grandmasters from every guild, the council were the most powerful group within the Order.

This meeting was nothing more than a formality, he told himself. The Order was obsessed with the past, trapped in rituals and traditions, and that was something he intended to change once he was in power.

As head of the Dreadnoughts he would effectively have

total control of the army, and only the Protectorate could offer any form of resistance, and he already had enough support from within their ranks to know it could be managed.

Jaeger had spent his entire career dreaming of an end to the constant threat of the maelstrom, and this was his chance of making it real. Once he was a member of the High Council, he would have access to all of the Order's most restricted knowledge and devices.

Including the Infinity Engine.

With the Infinity Engine, he would have the power to destroy the nightmares once and for all.

73

OPHELIA

In hindsight the crypt was a terrible idea, and they soon realised that there was nowhere to go once they were below stairs and with hardly any light.

Kaori and the cat sat amongst the stone tombs as Sabien searched for another way out.

'Okay, this is the point where you tell me you had a plan all along,' said Kaori, stroking Schrödinger's head.

Sabien had taken off his long leather coat and rolled up his sleeves. There were tattoos running down both his arms and Kaori remembered how the design ran across his chest and down his back, hiding the scar.

'I don't suppose you have a mirror on you?' he asked.

She shook her head.

The baying of the creatures echoed down the stone passage, and she felt Schrödinger's hackles raise — a sure sign that they'd broken through the first barricade.

Sabien unpacked every one of his weapons onto the top of a tomb. It was an impressive collection, but they both knew it wouldn't be enough.

'Any preference?' He waved his hand across the selection.

She picked up a stubby-looking pistol and felt the weight of it, then pulled out one of her own daggers and opted to stick with it.

'You're sure there's no other way?'

'They don't sound like they're in the mood for a conversation.'

Sabien picked up the gunsabre rifle and pulled out the magazine.

'We've got enough ammo for ten of them. Then it'll be down to blades and hand-to-hand,' he said, picking up a knife.

Sabien stared at himself in the dagger's silvered blade. He looked older, his hair shot through with white.

'How come you haven't aged?' he wondered, looking back at her.

She shrugged, trying out another pistol. 'Just good genes I guess.'

He went over and examined her face. 'No. This place isn't affecting you in the same way as me.'

A howl echoed down into the chamber as the first creature scrambled down the corridor.

Sabien sighted his gun and shot the creature through the head. A second monster leapt over the body of the first and it took two more shots to put it down. Lowering his gun, Sabien saw the darkened corridor was swarming with twisted, snarling horrors.

'You can't fight them all!' declared Kaori. 'You should leave.' She touched a wooden joist that held up the roof. 'I know you can weave with natural objects.'

He reloaded his rifle and hoisted it back into his shoulder. 'I'm not leaving you behind.'

The creatures crawled cautiously forwards over the bodies of their dead, eyes glowing in the dark.

'You don't have to protect me,' Kaori insisted, her voice sounding different somehow. 'Look at me, Michael.'

Sabien had never told her his first name. It was something only his mother used; the name of an Angel.

'How?' he asked, turning to face her.

Kaori was shrouded in a white smoke. Fluid shapes coalesced around her like oil in water, slowly solidifying into a beautiful, but intimidating, white dragon.

'I've been trying to find a way to tell you,' she said, her voice distorted by the sound of another.

'You're one of them?'

'No.'

The creature around her seemed to shudder and change. 'I'm not a Chimæra. This is a Ghast, a non-corporeal spirit. I had an accident a few years ago and it saved me. I've been co-existing with it ever since — her name is Ophelia, although gender is a little irrelevant.'

The shape around Kaori was growing more menacing with every second. Sharp fangs grew out from its ghostly jaws and long blades extended down her forearms.

'And Ophelia has weapons,' he observed, letting the rifle drop.

'Oh yes, but only in extreme circumstances.'

'Of course.'

Kaori smiled and the milky fog darkened until he could no longer see her face. The fearsome creature bolted towards the approaching monsters in a blur of scything blades and teeth.

Sabien looked down at Schrödinger, who sat with a contented look on his face.

'She's full of surprises isn't she?'

The cat looked up and Sabien wasn't sure if he didn't wink at him.

74

RESCUE

Caitlin tried to block out the sounds of the creatures that clawed and howled at the door. She was safe for now, but the rusting hinges were showing signs of give as the mortar around it began to crumble.

Her almanac was full of sketches from the walls, much of it written in languages that she couldn't decipher, but she knew if she could get back to Master Dorrowkind he would be able to make sense of it all.

Marcus had tried desperately to document everything he knew before he lost control. The scrawled marks on the walls were unclear, his muddled brain having switched between so many archaic languages it was impossible to know what it was.

Caitlin couldn't help but think about the conversation he had with her parents in the kitchen, and the fact that he had seemed to know what was going to happen to her. He had seen something in her future that was potentially going to kill her, but she had no idea what it could be.

'She won't survive without some kind of intervention.'

Suddenly, the building shook as if a bomb had just detonated outside. Caitlin fell to the floor, covering her head with her hands and praying the walls would hold. When she lifted her head, the air was full of dust and cordite, but at least the howls of the creatures had been silenced.

A series of loud clangs resounded from the other side of the door as the locks were broken and the bolts drawn back.

She crouched low, preparing herself to take out the first thing that came through the door.

The door burst open with such force that it swung completely off its hinges.

'Hello, kitkat!' said Rufius, standing in the doorway with a large sledgehammer — he looked like a scruffy Viking.

Rufius dropped the hammer and came over and picked her up. She hugged him tightly, the relief flooding through her as tears ran down her cheeks.

'Are you alright? Are you hurt?' he whispered. 'What on earth have you gotten yourself into?'

A squad of Dreadnoughts poured into the cell with their weapons drawn, followed by her godfather, who didn't look impressed at all.

'Caitlin Verity Makepiece,' he said and shook his head. 'What would your mother say?'

She ground her teeth and let go of Rufius. 'I think she would be rather proud of me actually!' she said, folding her arms and sticking her chin out a little.

'Would she now? And why would that be?'

'Do you know Commander Jaeger?'

He looked slightly taken aback by the name. 'I do, as a matter of fact. I should be attending his investiture right now, if I wasn't chasing down my wayward godchild.'

'He's in danger,' she said, pointing to the wall. 'The creature has one more target.'

75

INVESTITURE

The star chamber was empty, this was a closed session and the ranked seats that climbed up towards the ceiling were unusually silent.

The chamber was the closest thing the Order had to a government. The eight seats that sat at compass points around the circular floor were for the heads of each guild, but everyone had the right to speak when the Council was in session.

Today was not for the general population, today was an opportunity for the grandmasters to interrogate him and it was the nearest Jaeger had ever come to feeling like a criminal, perhaps because the chamber was used as a court as well as a debating room.

He stood at the centre of the golden star which had been set into the tiled floor — each point ended at a chair, the North pointing directly to the hooded figure of the founder.

'Colonel Jaeger,' announced the secretary of the court. 'You stand before the honoured members of the High Council as a candidate for the position of Commander-in-chief of the Draconian Defence Service.'

Jaeger nodded. 'I do.'

'The floor is open for questions,' the secretary said, sitting back down and taking out his quill.

The founder rose to his feet and walked onto the floor. 'I have one simple question for you commander. One that I hope you will answer honestly.'

There was something unusual about his voice. Jaeger had only met Lord Dee on two previous occasions and both times he had sounded like a benevolent old man.

'Would you submit to a seer?' he asked, pulling back the cowl.

Jaeger realised that it wasn't Lord Dee at all, but Edward Kelly, the Grand Seer.

Before he had a chance to react, Kelly had grabbed him by the wrist, his eyes burning with a dark intensity as he stared deep into his soul.

There was nowhere to hide from the probing mind of the Grand Seer. He scoured his timeline, opening locked and forgotten areas of his past that Jaeger had tried so hard to bury. Nothing he could do would stop the overpowering force of Kelly's mind.

When Kelly finally released him there was a look of mild amusement in his eyes.

'Well, what terrible secrets you keep,' he whispered with a knowing smile. 'Hell is empty and all the devils are here.'

'What is your verdict Grand Seer — is he worthy?' asked one of the seven guildmasters.

Kelly turned to face the council.

'He has done such things that would make the moon weep and chase the ebbing Neptune into night. There is rough magic here. But… ' — he held up one hand to silence them — 'the working of the mind discovers oft dark deeds in darkness schemed and he has worked so very darkly. He's exactly what you deserve — although for how long, who knows?'

With that he bowed to them and walked out of the chamber.

Jaeger let out a breath.

'Any other questions?' asked the secretary, a little confused by the Grand Seer's remarks.

They shook their head.

'Congratulations Commander, may I be the first to —'

Jaeger didn't wait for the rest of the speech, and turned to leave. There was something about the way Kelly had said: 'for how long', that bothered him. He hadn't been allowed to bring any guards or weapons into the chamber and he felt vulnerable without them.

The sooner he got back to his office the better.

76

THE LAKE

Caitlin and Rufius followed her godfather back through the ruins of the zoo. There were parts of bodies scattered across the enclosures, and the metal bars that contained them now lay twisted and bent out of their fittings.

'Looks like the lunatics have taken over the asylum,' Rufius mused.

'How did you know where I was?'

'Lyra showed me the mirror. She's a clever little minx.'

'I'm surprised she didn't insist on coming with you.'

He laughed. 'She did! We had to lock her up. Derado said it was far too dangerous to let a seer loose in here, let alone a recovering reaver — she's not happy.'

Caitlin smiled. He was right, this place was everything that Lyra should be kept away from. Her obsessions about the dead had nearly been the end of her. The malice of this place would have been too much for her sensitive soul.

'Where's Belsarus?'

Rufius shrugged. 'Haven't seen him since that disastrous presentation at the Royal Society.'

'He's been hiding here ever since, or at least part of him. He's insane — treats the creatures terribly. He threw me in with uncle Marcus, thinking he would eat me!'

Rufius turned around with a puzzled look on his face. 'Uncle Marcus?'

She nodded. 'Marcus is the creature. He's been altered by the maelstrom. He showed me some of what happened.'

Rufius tapped his temple. 'Don't remind me. I can still see the faces of the men that came back out of the breach.'

'There was hardly anything left of him,' Caitlin said despondently. 'Why didn't anyone tell me about him?'

Rufius scratched his beard. 'Well, firstly he was a bit of a black sheep, not someone that played nicely with others, and secondly he had gone dark. No one had seen him until he showed up that night at your parents' house. I think your dad believed he was dead, as it had been years. The Dreadnoughts can be a secretive bunch, and I think he was working for special operations.'

'He was a spy?'

Rufius shook his head. 'More like a lone wolf. Spent a lot of time out in the field. I've really no idea what he was up to.'

The lake was like a giant mirror, the Draconians had converted it into a portal and its surface reflected another sky — full of stars and a large pale moon.

As the others descended into the water, Rufius turned towards her.

'Did he tell you what happened to you parents?'

Caitlin shook her head. She'd considered telling Rufius about the conversation in the kitchen, but something held her back. The memories Marcus had shared were for her alone.

He had discovered something terrible, something that was going to kill her, and he'd made her parents leave because of it. She needed to know what it was.

77

TRUTH

The creature stood like a statue before him, as if it had been carved from one of his nightmares. Behind it the mirror through which the beast had just appeared remained black, its surface rippling like a lake on a moonless night.

The monster was truly hideous, but Jaeger felt no fear, and comforted himself with the fact that there were a dozen guards on the other side of his office door that would come to his aid in a second — should he call out.

But he didn't. Instead he studied it carefully, fascinated by the perfect embodiment of a killing machine — a useful weapon in the right hands.

Jaeger knew it was still partly human: revenge was a purely personal motivation, and what it had done to the other members of Project Osirion was clearly meant to send a message.

Sabien's reports were like the notes of a blind man wandering aimlessly through a massacre. The motive was plain to see — for those who knew all of the secrets, and there had been many. An entire garrison of Draconians lost to the failings of Jaeger's brainchild.

In retrospect, the project had been flawed from the beginning. Trying to get the various guilds to work together was always going to be fraught with problems, and perhaps that had been his biggest failing: believing that he could unite them.

He should have shut it down when Sergeant resigned. His chief engineer walking off the project was a clear sign that it was failing, but he was blind to their misgivings, deaf to the protests — all he could see was glory.

'It was supposed to rescue you,' he muttered, half-expecting some kind of response. 'How was I to know it would do this?'

The monster tilted its head first one way then the other, as if trying to understand what he was saying.

'They told me they'd tested it!' Jaeger lied, knowing very well that he'd rushed the production schedule to get a version out into the field. They were massively behind schedule and his superiors had already threatened to pull his funding. The QA department had complained incessantly about their inability to test it in real conditions, until he'd paid them off — everyone had a price, and it was just a question of finding their level.

'I'm your commanding officer,' he growled, pushing out his chest to show the many rows of medals. 'Remember, you're still a Dreadnought.'

The creature made a mock-salute and moved towards him.

78

STALEMATE

Belsarus was standing in the ballroom staring into the mirror, watching the world on the other side. A pale blue sky was breaking over the horizon, the sun painting the clouds with a hint of rosy gold.

'Such a wonderful view,' he said, and sighed, waving his hand across the scene and turning towards Sabien and Kaori.

She was still surrounded by the ghost-form of Ophelia, although no longer in her 'battle-state'. The creature enshrouded Kaori like a fine gossamer dress.

Sabien levelled a gun at Belsarus' head. 'Where's Caitlin?'

Belsarus smiled. 'The girl is with her uncle. I'm sure he's made quite a meal of her by now.' There was a hysterical undertone to his voice.

He was telling the truth. Sabien knew intuitively when someone was hiding something. Although it made no sense, Belsarus believed what he was saying.

'Where is she?' Kaori stepped forward, her ghost taking a more offensive posture, its horns coalescing over her head.

'Well, isn't that a sight?' Belsarus marvelled at the armoured being. 'A non-corporeal transformation — so much more elegant than these hideous types,' he said, waving his hand toward the shadows.

With that a monster came crashing out of the dark and knocked Sabien's gun from his hand, sending both him and the weapon across the floor.

'Caliban doesn't have any of your finesse I'm afraid, but he still has his uses.'

The disfigured creature picked up Sabien by the neck and held a blade against it with a deformed hand.

'Can I master? Can I cut it?'

Belsarus held up a hand to stay the execution.

'What do you say, my dear? My life for his? Sounds like a fair deal doesn't it?'

Ophelia was flexing her form. New and more menacing configurations transformed her body as Kaori imagined all the ways in which she would hurt Belsarus.

'I assume you still have some modicum of control of your symbiont?'

Kaori gritted her teeth and the antagonistic form retreated, returning to a more serene shape.

'Good girl,' he said through a sneer. 'Now, be so kind as to tell me how my friend Dangerfield is doing. I believe he's heading up the Xenobiology department these days.'

'He's dead,' growled Sabien. 'One of your creatures killed him.'

Belsarus frowned and motioned to Caliban, who pushed the jagged blade into Sabien's skin until blood ran down the edge

'I wasn't talking to you, boy.'

'He's telling the truth, I saw it,' pleaded Kaori. 'There was a symbol carved into his chest.'

Belsarus' gaze turned towards her. 'What kind of symbol?'

'Jailer.'

He nodded, repeating the word silently, his eyes glazing over slightly.

Kaori glanced over at Sabien. Caliban had wrapped his twisted limbs around him, the dagger dangerously close to Sabien's carotid artery. He was concentrating on his master, whilst Sabien's eyes were trying to tell her something, but she couldn't understand what it was.

'Marcus was always one of my most difficult patients,' said Belsarus.

79

THE REAL MEMORY

Jaeger felt the creature's mind infiltrate his as the claws punctured his temples and it made a connection.

It was Marcus. There was no doubt after the moment the intuit was established.

HELLO SIR. REMEMBER ME?

The message was like an unspoken voice inside his skull. Jaeger surrendered to the powerful probe as it drilled down into his mind. Like a dark root it burrowed through his memories, searching for something, spreading like a virus along his neural pathways.

WHERE IS IT?

The thought appeared.

SHOW ME THE REASON.

He offered no resistance as the thing ransacked his past, tearing open so many forgotten areas until it found it. The locked door buried deep within his past.

OPEN.

Images of terrible things flashed in front of him as

Marcus showed Jaeger all the ways in which he might die. The colonel felt his nerves catch fire, pain lancing through his body as Marcus shared some of his own suffering. It was a threat of things that may happen if he didn't comply.

Jaeger relinquished the memory, unlocking the door to that time.

He was in a room full of people, who were sitting around a large mahogany boardroom table with plans and notes scattered across it, the stoic expressions on their faces implying it had been a long and tedious session.

As project director, Jaeger sat at the head of the table, Henery Sergeant to his left and Dangerfield on his right.

'We've lost over thirty men in the last six weeks. This can't go on,' said one of the generals from the other end of the table.

Marcus recognised the battalion commanders, but there were others, and from their robes it was clear they were masters of the other guilds.

'The maelstrom is growing more active with every day,' added one of the Copernicans. 'We need to know why. We need data!'

'The Dreadnoughts were created to protect the continuum, not investigate it,' complained one of the Draconian officers. 'We've lost too many to the damn breaches as it is. I won't send good men into it.'

'What about bad ones?' Jaeger suggested.

'Criminals?'

'Mavericks of one sort or another. There are a few specialists that spring to mind.'

There was a general rumble of discontented discussion.

'The Copernicans could not condone such activity.'

'Nor the Scriptoria.'

Jaeger stood up and pressed his knuckles down into the table. 'What I'm proposing doesn't require your approval. You need something that requires a special unit, one that can cross back and forth into the maelstrom. I believe we have just the kind of technology to facilitate that.' He clapped Henery on the shoulder.

'It's known as Project Osirion. We've been working with the Antiquarians on it for the last five years.'

An image appeared on the wall behind him: a three-dimensional projection of the back-pack and breastplate appeared, rotating slowly.

'It's a salvation device, a temporal parachute, which will quite literally pull you back from the brink of hell.'

The room went quiet, everyone studying the device as statistics and specifications scrolled across it.

'My engineers tell me it will be ready for active service in under two months. I'm putting together a team of specialists to take it into the second dynasty and deal with the Osirion issue.'

The room stood in unison and applauded.

Jaeger smiled and soaked up the praise. Henery Sergeant, however, was not smiling. He was glaring at the man.

Sergeant waited until everyone had left.

'I said two years!'

Jaeger shook his head. 'We haven't got two years. The whole bloody continuum will be overrun by then.'

'But it needs to be field tested.'

'And that's exactly what I'm suggesting.'

'And who are the team of specialists?'

Jaeger smiled. 'Renegades, like Marcus Makepiece. Special operations have more than a few who would volunteer for such a mission.'

'But it's suicide!'

'Not if your device works. You need to have more faith in your work.'

Sergeant stood up, his eyes full of fire. 'My device will work fine, but it needs to be tested in the field. We have no idea how the maelstrom will alter the outcome.'

'Do you have a better option? Who else can report back on what they find on the other side?'

Sergeant looked dismayed. 'I can't be part of this,' he said, picking up his notes and handing them to Jaeger. 'This is all on you now. We're working in the dark and you don't even want to light a match first. I won't be the one who sends them to their deaths.'

'They're Dreadnoughts. They know their destiny.'

The memory closed abruptly and Jaeger opened his eyes. The creature was standing over him, its claws moving away from his face and tearing open his uniform.

'It was necessary, don't you understand?' he pleaded as he felt the first claw penetrate his skin.

'No,' came a dark and menacing voice.

A shot rang out and a red rose blossomed on the creature's chest.

'Marcus, no!' screamed Caitlin.

The creature turned towards her voice, its teeth bared like a feral cat.

Caitlin was running towards them, leaving behind the Dreadnoughts who were pointing fearsome looking guns at him.

She caught the creature as it toppled off Jaeger and onto the floor, cradling his head in her lap like a lover.

'I know what he did, Marcus.'

A blood-stained, clawed hand wrapped itself around one of hers and placed it on his temple.

Suddenly they were in the kitchen with her parents once more.

'Why can't we tell her?' her mother was shouting at Marcus.

'To know changes the outcome,' Marcus warned. 'You know the fundamental rules of prediction. I can only guarantee her safety if she's unaware.'

'Do you know who the Paradox is?'

Marcus shook his head. 'No, nor when it will arrive. All I know is that Caitlin will be an important factor in the intervention.'

Her parents stared at each other, tears welling in their eyes as they silently shared a moment of grief.

'When do we have to go?' her father asked without taking his eyes off Caitlin's mother.

'Tomorrow.'

80

GRAVITY ENGINES

The sounds of the explosions rocked the ballroom, shaking dust out of the broken ceiling and rattling the chandeliers.

'It appears we have visitors,' said Belsarus, walking towards Kaori. He was carrying something in both hands; a small spinning sphere, like a globe.

'I don't have time to explain the physics of what is about to occur, which is a shame, because they took me a lifetime to perfect.' His eyes became wistful. 'The first version of this nearly took over the entire ballroom — I've made a few improvements since then.'

Kaori could hear Caliban panting with excitement. Whatever Belsarus was going to do, his monster was becoming more unpredictable with every second.

'This is my finest achievement. A gravity engine — the fabled perpetual motion machine.'

The air around the sphere was beginning to vibrate as its spin increased. 'It uses gravity wells to distort space and time. I won't bore you with the details, but this tiny sphere can take me anywhere in the continuum in the blink of an *eye*.' He accentuated the last word like a Vegas show magician.

He held the sphere in front of her face. Ophelia retreated from the oscillating waves, folding herself back inside Kaori's body.

'As I suspected, the fields are an anathema to storm-kin.'

Kaori looked to Sabien, unable to mask the pain the device was inflicting on her — it was like she was being torn in two.

Sabien took his cue and drove his elbow deep into Caliban's solar plexus. The creature coughed and heaved, vomiting dark bile onto the floor. Sabien kicked out, knocking him over, but he was stronger than he looked and rolled back up to his feet, slashing the gruesome blade in wild, scything motions.

As Belsarus reached out to grab Kaori, there was a familiar growl from behind her, and a flash of teeth and fur as Schrödinger launched himself at the old man. His jaw closed around the outstretched arm and took him down onto the floor.

The gravity engine span off across the room and Kaori felt its effects dissipating. Ophelia reasserted herself and they charged at Caliban, running him through with a translucent set of horns and driving him into the nearest wall.

Sabien went to check on Belsarus. Schrödinger had his jaws clamped around his neck, applying just enough pressure to ensure compliance but not enough to choke him.

'You're under arrest,' Sabien informed him, collapsing down onto his knees beside him.

He patted the sabre-tooth. 'Constable, read him his rights.'

Schrödinger growled.

81

DEPARTMENT OF SHADOWS

[Royal Zoological Gardens, London. Date: 11.828]

Kaori was supervising the finishing touches to the gateway of her new department when Sabien found her.

'The Delawney Dimension,' he read off the plaque on the large round mirror that stood in the middle of the room. 'It has a nice ring to it.'

He ruffled Schrödinger's neck as the cat rubbed his head up and down his leg.

'I preferred it to the "Department of Shadows", and she deserves to be remembered for her discovery — even if it was fatal.'

The mirror was suspended in a large brass frame in the middle of the circular room, with twelve glass-fronted chambers set into the walls around it. In each of the cells was a unique specimen of Chimæra, their bodies ravaged by the maelstrom. Graphical overlays flickered on the cell doors, showing life-sign readouts and three-dimensional models of their separate life-forms.

'Lieutenant Davies MacTeague,' he read aloud. 'And a Vazidoajl?' He struggled with the pronunciation.

'A Vashi-doa,' she corrected phonetically. 'The last two consonants are silent.'

'Are they're alive?'

'In stasis—at least until we can figure out how to separate them. Which may take a while.'

'And the shadow dimension?' asked Sabien, staring at the black mirror.

'Closed until further notice. The Antiquarians are looking into using it for storage of non-perishables, but it's off-limits until we've done a thorough sweep.'

'Good plan.'

'So, have you closed the case?'

Sabien nodded. 'Jaeger was indicted under article thirty, and he's serving two consecutive terms for perverting the course of justice, fraud and wilful dereliction of duty.'

'Not for murder?'

Sabien shrugged. 'It's hard to prove when virtually everyone involved in the conspiracy is dead. The chief inquisitor believes his defence could've argued that it was a time of war and there are a whole bunch of laws that absolve commanding officers from the deaths caused under their authority.'

'What about Belsarus?'

'Medics tried to recover his body, but failed. It didn't survive the transition back through the mirror. They've managed to save his mind though. He's been donated to the Antiquarian engineering institute.'

Kaori sighed. 'All that work and we're still no closer to understanding how to survive in the maelstrom.'

'That's why we need your department,' he said, realising he was quoting her rationale. 'Surely the Chimæra must give you some kind of clue?'

She shrugged, 'Maybe — too early to say.'

'Ever the pessimist, but I hear congratulations are in order,' he said, producing a bottle of champagne.

Kaori blushed. 'Don't make a big thing out of it.'

'Head of Xenobiology? Sounds big to me.'

She scowled at him, and the outline of small white fangs appeared in front of her face.

'Okay,' — he held up his hands in mock surrender — 'no need to get Ophelia involved.'

She smiled, and they dissipated away like smoke.

'So where are we going for dinner?' she asked, threading her arm through his.

'I thought I'd cook,' he replied, walking towards the stairs.

'You can cook?'

82

HISTORIAN

Master Dorrowkind was fast asleep, his feet up on the desk with a book resting on his enormous stomach that rose and fell slowly with his deep, resinous snoring.

Caitlin coughed lightly and his eyes fluttered open, myopically searching the room for whatever had disturbed him.

'Good afternoon, Sir.'

He swung his feet off the desk and in the process managed to dislodge the book and his glasses that were perched high on his forehead. He waved his hands around in a pathetic effort to catch them.

'Makepiece, what have I told you about disturbing me when I'm studying?' he stuttered, picking them both up off the floor.

'Sorry, Sir, but we have a tutorial — my final dissertation?'

'Ah yes, the Mayerstein indexation.'

Caitlin took the document out of her bag and passed it to him. 'Not exactly.'

'The Tempest — the mirrored world of Johannes Belsarus?' Dorrowkind read the title aloud.

'There have been a few changes since we last spoke. I've decided I don't want to be an Archivist.'

'You don't?' he asked, his eyes narrowing.

'Nor do I want to be a Draconian — not yet anyway,' she continued, crossing her arms defiantly. 'You taught me that the mission of the Scriptoria was to preserve knowledge, so that we aren't doomed to repeat the mistakes of the past.'

He nodded sternly. 'Indeed it is.'

'And to achieve this we must do everything in our power to ensure the past is documented. Well, I've decided my skills are best served in research — I wish to be a Historian. I want to write about our history, not just find the lost books of forgotten civilisations.'

Dorrowkind's face cracked and a wide smile broke across his face. 'Congratulations, Miss Makepiece, I believe you have passed.' He handed her back her dissertation without opening it.

Caitlin took it with a nod, then turned and left. She waited until she was safely out of his view before laughing and punching the air.

83

BEACH

[Koh Samui, Thailand. Date: 11.210]

Caitlin felt the warmth of the sun on her skin and the cool sand under her toes. Waves were gently washing up the beach — lulling her to sleep.

Somewhere, further along the shore, she could hear Lyra and Sim arguing. They had been on Koh Samui for the last ten days — it was Caitlin's choice. The thirteenth-century island was unspoilt and unpopulated. Sim hated beaches, and had decided to explore the island, while Lyra had spent most of the time collecting shells and plaiting Caitlin's hair — when she wasn't trying to communicate with the dolphins.

As the two approached her, their voices reduced to a whisper. Caitlin pretended to be asleep, her face hidden beneath a straw hat that Lyra had made out of palm leaves.

'Shall we tell her?' asked Sim.

'I think she's had enough excitement this month. We promised we'd let her relax, remember?'

'Yeah, but this is really cool. It's not often you find evidence of a lost civilisation.'

'You get to name it you know.'

He chuckled. 'I don't think the 'Simians' sounds like a very advanced culture, do you?'

'No,' she giggled. 'Nor does the 'De Friesans'.'

'Sounds like a herd of cows,' said Caitlin, tipping the brim of the hat back to look at them.

The sun had browned both of their skins and bleached their hair. They looked like castaways in their sarongs. Lyra had a beautiful white flower in her hair, and Sim was still soaking wet from the sea.

'What have you found, exactly?'

'A cave,' Lyra tutted.

'A cave full of charts,' he corrected her.

'Sea charts?' Caitlin sat up.

Sim nodded. 'Evidence of ancient maritime activity.'

'Show me,' she said, standing up and brushing off the sand.

'Are you sure?' asked Lyra.

'Yeah, it's got to be better than lying here trying to figure out who the Paradox is going to be.'

Lyra put one of her flowers into Caitlin's hair. 'Oh, I have the feeling he's going to be a handsome, intelligent man with stars in his eyes.'

Sim scoffed, picking up their things. 'Riding a unicorn perhaps? Everyone knows the Paradox is a myth. There's no statistical evidence — Hey, wait for me!'

The girls had already started up the beach.

EPILOGUE

The founder sat opposite Rufius, the two staring at each other across the desk like chess opponents.

'Who's going to do it?'

'Kelly, of course, there's no one better.'

Rufius grimaced at the sound of his name. 'The man is half-mad. What about young Eckhart? Much as I hate the arrogant arse, I'm told Dalton's shaping up to be a fine redactor, and she knows him.'

The founder shook his head. 'No, he's too inexperienced. This needs a very light touch by someone with a steady hand. Caitlin must never know anything has changed.'

Rufius scratched at his beard. 'And the Copernicans believe that redaction is the only way?'

Dee's expression hardened into one of grim determination. 'The memories of Marcus must be removed. It changes her motivation. She becomes obsessed with the Paradox, and trying to understand what her uncle had discovered that would lead to her death. Eventually her lack of progress makes her unhappy and unfulfilled. The chances of suicide within the next five years are currently over seventy percent.'

Rufius nodded. 'Then I agree. We can't let that happen. When will he do it?'

The founder waved a hand at a letter that sat on his desk. 'As soon as I sign the order.'

Rufius stood up to leave. 'And Marcus? Have they managed to save him?'

'He's in stasis, although there's very little left of him. Kelly says the memories that he collected from his victims make for quite a compelling case. It was as though he were trying to gather all of the elements that led to his accident together, leaving us with a chilling legacy. Jaeger had become obsessed with destroying the maelstrom, and Kelly tells me he even had designs on using the Infinity Engine as a weapon.'

They both grimaced at the thought of what that would mean.

'He had a great deal of support for Project Osirion. The real failure was that we didn't learn from the mistakes. Burying the truth only leads to repeating the errors of the past. Dangerfield and Sergeant were brilliant men, and they will be greatly missed.'

'And Belsarus?'

'I have instructed the Scriptorians to confiscate all copies of his work. Much as I hate to lock books away, sometimes knowledge truly is a dangerous thing. I have also asked Grandmaster Derado to order a full review of the Dreadnought's special operations. There are too many secrets within this Order for my liking.'

ALSO BY ANDREW HASTIE

Caitlin returns in Anachronist

Buy now on Amazon

ACKNOWLEDGMENTS

Thanks to everyone who continues to support me on this journey. You're all amazing, but most of all to Karen and the girls — who I've bored senseless with my constant plot-related questions — it will be worth it I promise!

To all those who have read this and given me feedback (including my new beta team!) — without you these books would be unreadable piles of confusing nonsense. I thank you for your time and will be buying you beer-related gifts shortly.

This book was originally written as part of NaNoWriMo. If you haven't heard of it, go look it up — it's a great idea and celebrates writing in all its wonderful craziness.

ABOUT THE AUTHOR

For more information about Andy and The Infinity Engines series please visit: www.infinityengines.com

Please don't forget to leave a review!
Thank you!
Andy x

Printed in Great Britain
by Amazon